ABOUT *Max Turns Yellow*

Martha King's riveting mystery, *Max Turns Yellow*, is an impossible-to-put-down yarn involving two separate stories that get braided together into one frightening whole that entwines a weirdly dysfunctional family and a murder – and both threads involve the written word. I should point out that this entire strange, sad mélange takes place in New York City; Vinegar Hill, to be exact, though other boroughs figure in it too. Martha King knows her city backwards and forwards; and she understands the ins and outs of financial shenanigans as well. Though the book is set in the 1980's, it resonates with the current situation our country is in all too well! *Max Turns Yellow* is a must read!

—**Ron Kolm**, editor of *Sensitive Skin*, author of *Swimming in the Shallow End*

I know it's a cliché to say I couldn't put it down, but *Max Turns Yellow* carried me so effortlessly along, I finished it in two sittings. Honestly, it's been awhile since I've enjoyed a book as much as this one. And, as a writer myself, I'm kind of in awe of how it begins; it just drew me in before I even knew what happened, and I was delighted.

—**Don Yorty**, author of *Spring Sonnets*

Another page-turner from Martha King. This second book in the MAX series is set in Brooklyn's famous Vinegar Hill as well as in the middle of a major cancer research center in Manhattan. Ms. King once again thrusts the reader into her protagonist's specific geographic space and puts him or her among New York's downtown artists, writers, and hangers-on. And again this entertainment offers much to think about.

—**Patricia Ryan**, author of *Living with the Brooklyn Bridge*

Max is back and the mayhem is spreading. Martha King's artist detective once again finds himself in the center of a web of violence and intrigue when the brother of his partner, Britz, lands in big trouble after getting busted for publishing a dead man's manuscript as his own. When Britz turns up dead, Max sets out to find her killer. Notable for King's intimate knowledge of the bohemian art scene in Brooklyn in the 60s, *Max Turns Yellow* is an intricately plotted page-turner that will keep you guessing even as it delights you with its nostalgic portrait of a long vanished Brooklyn.

—**Michael Boughn**, author of *Business As Usual*

With a sharp eye for detail that's always true to its time and place, Martha King delivers a mystery set firmly in the psychological. Her lived knowledge of the tribal New York art world informs this chronicle of how camaraderie, blood ties and bohemian domesticity can become dislodged by rivalries, rumor, and the shifting alliances of being *Outside/Inside*, the title of her excellent memoir. In this second volume of her *Max* trilogy, after *Max Sees Red*, King creates another riveting ride with her complex protagonist at the center of a disparate group of eccentric, flawed and risk-taking characters. This reader awaits the third and final installment with great anticipation.

—**Bonny Finberg**, author of *Kali's Day*

Max Turns Yellow...begins with a shocker, is filled with unexpected but plausible twists that keep piling up, has moments of real menace (especially in relation to the Mafia's hangout), and there are times when suspense is ratcheted up to exquisite heights..... She has supplied a taut story...while offering a profundity of theme and character that goes beyond generic [crime fiction] expectations.

—**Jim Feast**

Max Turns Yellow
BROOKLYN, 1986

Martha King

SPUYTEN DUYVIL
NEW YORK CITY

This book is a work of fiction. Names, characters, places, and incidents are used fictitiously or are the product of the author's imagination. Any resemblance to actual persons, living or dead, is coincidental. However, the author would like to thank many friends and associates for inspiring the events and characters. I couldn't have invented all of it without help.

I am also deeply grateful to Bonny Finberg for her exquisite editorial review, Eileen Tabios who published a chapter in her blog "Making the Novel", and Sanjay Agnihotri who published the opening chapter in his fine magazine *Local Knowledge*. Other early readers and advisors include Sansana Sawasdikosol, Earl Heuer, Shelly Marlow, Mitch Highfill, Michael Seth Stuart, and Kim Lyons. And of course, as ever, my first reader and dear supporter, Basil King.

ISBN 978-1-952419-44-7
Cover: Brooklyn Bridge c. 1980

Library of Congress Cataloging-in-Publication Data

Names: King, Martha, 1937- author.
Title: Max turns yellow : Brooklyn, 1986 / Martha King.
Description: New York City : Spuyten Duyvil, [2020] |
Identifiers: LCCN 2020044688 | ISBN 9781952419447 (paperback)
Subjects: GSAFD: Mystery fiction.
Classification: LCC PS3561.I4817 M394 2020 | DDC 813/.54--dc23
LC record available at https://lccn.loc.gov/2020044688

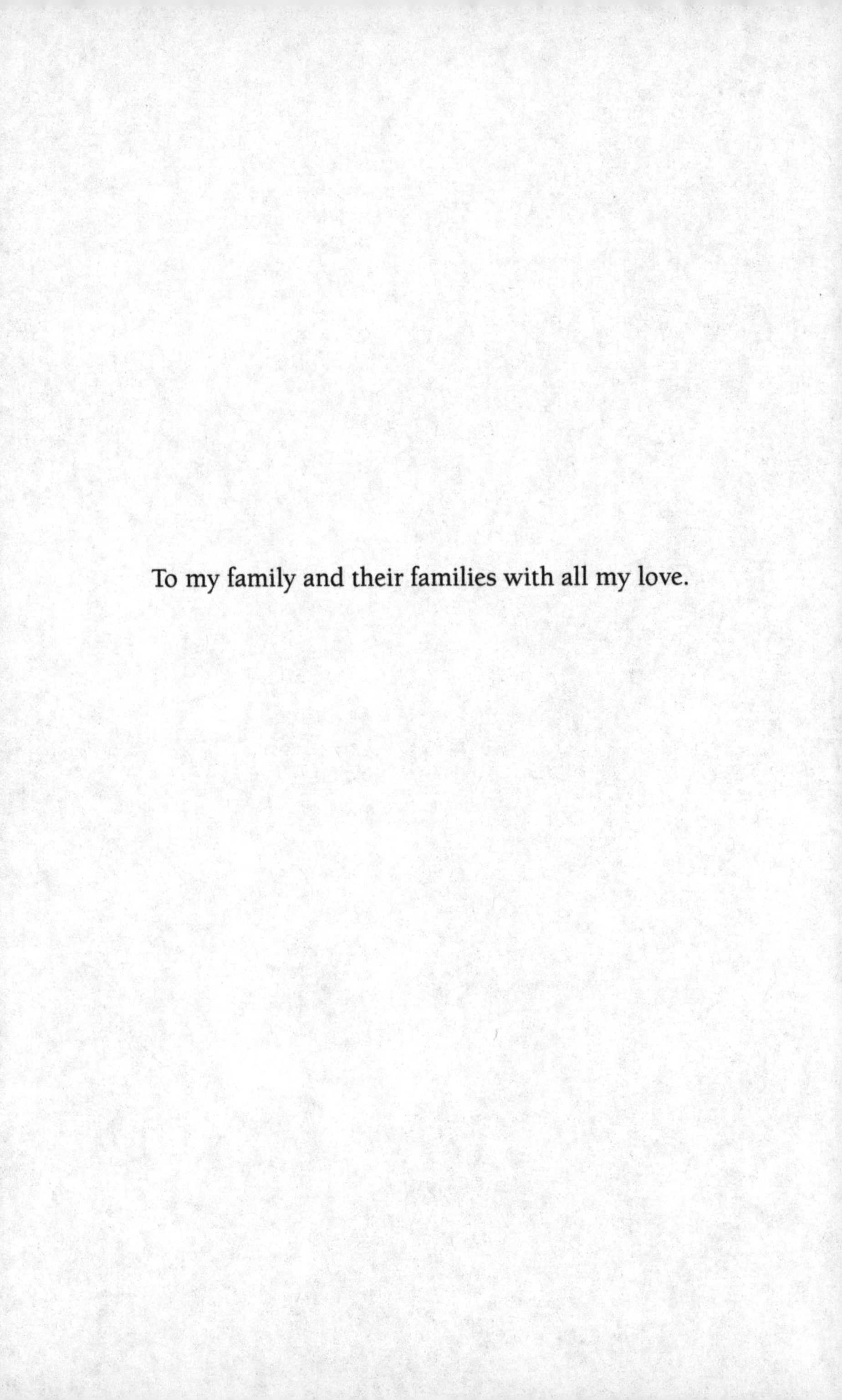

To my family and their families with all my love.

MAX TURNS YELLOW

Prelude
(in place of an epigraph)

Double Indemnity has already been used.
Ship of Fools has already been used.
House of Mirth has already been used.

Plus we know a lot about greed.
That is we know what we'd do if we *really* believed
no one else would ever find out.
Martha King

A DINNER DATE

So now we have Theo, thin, skinny, pale, a coward's coward if he could ever be open enough with anyone to expose his cowardice. Not Theo Henneberg! He hides it very well. He's the boy who reads a lot. He's the boy who hates sports. In school he was the one who spoke only when he had to, only when he was called on, only when it was demanded.

Theo sometimes wonders if he'd be better off as a girl; he envies what is expected of women in contrast to what everyone seems to expect of men. He doesn't think he's sexually queer: men don't turn him on. In fact, the three times he tried it, he found sex with men too damn rough. All that pinching and punching, the love bites, the massive bangs into his asshole or throat. He wants sex gentled. He wants to be a girl with another girl. To cuddle and stroke. To think and lick and slowly coax out the tingles.

Theo is going to find James, dead, in the sub-basement just below James' study in the basement. James' study is a room below street level in a Lower East Side tenement building. It's in the front and has a single six-inch high window, high on the wall, and so streaked with silt it barely admits any light at all. The room is thickly lined with books stacked in towers of orange plastic milk crates, floor to ceiling. The crates encircle his flat plank desk. His little haven is reached down a short flight of steps, guarded on the sidewalk level by a low fence and an inward opening gate. Inside, the door to a sub-basement below James' workroom has no lock. It is usually latched.

Theo will wonder why James left it unlatched. He'll wonder what James was looking for.

James left the flossy French restaurant on the first floor of the tenement building next door, large cloth napkin to his mouth, smothering his wheezing. He'd left his dinner companions, Beth and Rose Ann. He'd fled for his sanctuary next door where he'd have the freedom to retch, wheeze, cough, and gag without restraint. Boeuf bourguignon, who'd expect it? Was it gristle? It couldn't be bone!

But no gag came.

§

Upstairs next door, Beth and Rose Ann went on sitting at their small table, mystified but not so alarmed that they didn't continue eating. The beef was beautifully soft from its long simmer in red wine. A faint whiff of smoked bacon emerged, Beth noted. Little pearl onions floated in the dark gravy. When they'd finished and James had still not returned, they talked about how mercurial he could be. Had he left them without a word? He was known for doing things like that.

"This is plenty annoying," Beth looked fondly at her partner who shared her exasperation. James had invited them. They'd naturally expected him to pick up the check. A restaurant this expensive would not—with their carefully monitored budget—be their normal choice. They didn't have to discuss their shared intention to skip a salad or coffee or dessert. Now with James still absent it was clearly time to split.

"I'll put it on mine," Rose Ann said fishing out her charge card. "We'll figure it out later."

"Fuck him," Beth said. "Just fuck him." Being disappointed by a man was such a damn cliché for both of them. Boring, boring, boring.

§

James was there on the dirt floor at the foot of the raw plank steps. He was there, dead, his face engorged and blackened. From suffocation or from the fall? Had the fall killed him? Did he have a crushed windpipe? A rib bone piercing his lung? Or was it simply that gob of food blocking his windpipe and stilling his breath forever?

Theo had first tapped his foot against the tiny basement window because he could make out that a light was on inside. Nothing. In the hallway the study door swung open at the first sharp knock. Was he expected? James had told him, "Come by after twelve." James, he hoped, was going to give him advice about submitting his short stories. Or he was going to make a move. Theo didn't know, but both possibilities were okay. He'd been one of James' students in a short story workshop at the New School, and he was both flattered and suspicious of James' indications of interest. A midnight appointment wasn't weird. Theo lived four blocks away and as he later had to explain to the cops, he worked a night job doing the books for the Loisasida Theater on Rivington.

As soon as Theo entered he saw the sub-basement door hanging open. It was dark below. He found the wall switch at the top of the stair.

3

He looked for a long minute and then sat where he was, on the top step. James' head was cocked at a lethal angle and his face was slack and grey as stone. All around the dead man was a snowstorm of manuscript papers. Had James pulled at something from above as he fell? There were storage shelves lining the walls above the stairway. Theo reached down and picked up a page. Then he did what he always did when he was frightened. He began to read.

§

It was much later when he got up and retrieved the remainder of the spilled pages, which had fallen not on the steps but on the sub-basement floor. This entailed carefully stepping around James. Theo also picked up a purple paper file folder that had clearly held the papers, returned to his perch on the top step and put all the pages into order inside it. Deeply concentrating, he read what he had missed. Smell made him move at last. It was not putrefaction. Death had relaxed James' internal sphincters releasing the contents of bowels and bladder. Theo buttoned his overcoat and stashed the file in his leather shoulder bag.

It was six a.m. early spring dawn. The slit window glowed a dirty blue.

He used James' landline to call 911.

"I've just found my friend on the basement stairs. Please come as soon as you can. He's totally dead." He gave the address and his name and went to the door to wait.

<blockquote>
On one occasion, in 1870, the Army destroyed stills that were capable of churning out 250 barrels of alcohol each day—a volume worth $5,000 in unpaid taxes (equivalent to $99,066 in 2018). The battles between the government and the neighborhood became known as the 'Whisky Wars' and left the residents of Vinegar Hill suspicious of outsiders.

—*Wikipedia*
</blockquote>

PUBLICATION PARTY, VINEGAR HILL

The F Train stop at York Avenue was totally empty. No surprise. At 7 p.m. on a Saturday evening in 1986 almost no one was ever there. Tonight was just a little different. A small gang of friends disgorged from the Brooklyn bound train and poured onto the silent platform. Giggling and broken bits of banter were answered by tunnel echoes. It's a long two-track tunnel with a narrow concrete island for passengers in the middle and only one exit. Halfway toward the dead end a small call box for summoning help is affixed to a support column. With a little red light like a Christmas tree bulb. Theo preferred not to think how it might help if toughs, or even one tough, were on the platform between the call box and the only way out.

Nothing to worry tonight as seven people marched their cheerful party-noise up the exit stair led by Max Birtwhistle, painter and the party host. He and Theo Henneberg had planned this to follow the formal presentation of Theo's just published novel at the Gotham Book Mart. Max is one of Theo's closest friends, or does Max think of himself as Theo's mentor? There's something a bit big-brother about his attitude—and Theo loves it. The rest the group have never been to Max's new outpost in Brooklyn. Foreign territory Brooklyn is. Most of them are denizens of the Lower East Side or of what's left of SoHo. But when a prominent painter up and purchases a whole building in a previously unknown neighborhood, it's not only a signal that he's selling his work at a brisk pace, it's a chance for all his friends to scout out a new part of town and a great kick to be invited to an affair that promises copious food and drink.

The Gotham's upstairs event room had been hot, over-crowded, and filled with what insiders like to call "influencers". Theo's agent had circled like a raptor ensuring that Theo had had to endure enthusiastic introductions. Max grinned watching this, knowing the drill from his many gallery openings. "Hang in there, sweetie," he'd muttered passing Theo on his way to the john.

"So this is Vinegar Hill? What a desert! Where can you get beer?" Bill's snazzy party duds looked eerie on the empty cobblestoned street that plunged downhill to the very faintly shining East River. Bill was sporting a large western hat, a fringed waistcoat, and a gaudy bandanna—fruits of his latest venture doctoring TV scripts uptown.

The looming warehouses and buildings on Front Street were completely dark. Either deserted or locked shut for the weekend.

"Well actually that's called Dumbo. The place I bought's a few blocks over. Either way you have to go all the way to Myrtle to buy much of anything," Max announced, "but I've got a full fridge. Besides, Britz is cooking. I told you she's expecting us." He was in a full proprietary mode, his favorite suede jacket open to the January wind, his head hatless, and his loose gray hair riffling in the brisk river wind.

"She didn't want to be at the Gotham? Your own sister?" This from Lois to Theo. "I wondered where she was." Lois has been Theo's friend for more than ten years. She's nearly 60 now, with a pony tail of stringy once-brown hair and a shadow raked face but her youthful anger hasn't subsided. Not a bit. She had once worked for the pioneering sexologist Wilheim Reich and was held in some awe by younger radicals. She could tell harrowing stories about Dr. Reich's persecution by the feds. She'd been with him when he was forced to watch the burning of his research papers in the Rangeley, Maine municipal incinerator.

"Yep, our government sponsored book-burning," she'd inform her listeners. Max knew she relished her punch line: "All the rest was burnt to cinders on Gansevoort Pier right here in liberal New York City."

Max figured on needling her back: "S'okay, Lois. So, how's Ho?"

Blank look from Lois.

"Ho Chi Min!"

"Damnation. Old Ho. The vet says he has kidney failure. The vet wants me to put him on dialysis. Dialysis! For a dog. True, only way to get him down the stairs for a pee is to carry him, and then a pee takes forever. Honestly Max, he won't be much longer..."

"Oh Lois, I'm so sorry." He tried to put a brotherly arm across her sharp shoulders. She shook him off and pulled her army surplus jacket tighter.

"Yeah. Hate to lose him. But Jesus Christ, he's almost

sixteen. And I don't want to tell you what they'd charge. He's a *dog*! Dialysis for dogs. It's just plain immoral."

They paused on a dark corner, opposite humming machinery in a sprawling Con Edison storage yard guarded by chain-link fencing. The little parade waited for stragglers.

"It's just up this street," Max called out. "Turn right at that alley. My place is in the back."

Everyone except Dora walked rapidly up the broken street, beyond eager to get some place warm and light. Dora grabbed Lois's arm.

"Whaja mean 'immoral'—he's your *companion*. You owe him the longest life he can have." Behind enormous eyeglass frames, Dora's eyes brimmed seriousness.

"Are you nuts? Even if it didn't cost the earth, you think I'm gonna lug my sick old dog all the way up to 34th Street and make him sit through hours of IV's? Damn straight it's immoral!"

"Lois! Love is love. This would save his life!"

"Honest to God, you've been a social worker too damn long," Lois roared shaking free of Dora's hand. "Kids with lead poisoning waiting months for a public health nurse appointment. *That's* immoral."

"Ladies, please!" Theo was almost wailing. "This is my book party. Please!

"Max wants us to just cool it after all that Gotham Book Mart kerfuffle."

"Yeah, kerfuffle," Bob said, straightening out the wind-blown fringes of his vest. "You got critics humming money songs at you. You got a profile in the fucking *New York Times* coming up. A year ago you were temping for minibucks. I wouldn't mind a kerfuffle like that."

"Children, children," Max announced turning keys on the locks of the heavy wooden door to a low-lying industrial building.

Lights were on inside—low bridge lamps in a wide front area holding a motley collection of well-used sofas, easy chairs, and side tables—with brilliant track lights across the wider back part where Max painted and made his huge collage constructions. A kitchen area with new butcher-block counters went halfway the length of a windowless wall on the street side. Beyond it a hallway and partitions suggested more. A room for silkscreens. A room for sleeping. A sky-lit bathroom with shower, tub, and sinks.

"Christ this is huge!" thrilled Rose Ann.

"It was a pickle warehouse," Max explained. "Man it took a lot to get that pickle reek out. But it has great floors." They were. Nineteenth century planks of heavy oak. Trees that had lived a hundred years until logged and rafted down the Hudson to lumber yards in Queens. Planks strong enough to hold 1200 barrels of pickled cucumbers for a thousand delis and lunch counters across the city.

"Where's Betsy?" Rose Ann whispered to Beth. Everyone knew Betsy had been Max's partner since forever.

"Shit, Rose Ann, it was over a year ago. She took off with Alex. The potter with the place on Baxter Street? They've gone into production potting together. They make hundreds of sets of all the same stuff. Alex got contracts from department store chains. Crazy stuff," Beth said.

"I need a drink," said Rose Ann, wrinkling her nose.

"Yeah, don't look so disgusted. It gets worse. They moved down to Philly and I hear they hire a lot of Asians, illegals, women mostly. Teach 'em to paint identical designs, smeared just enough to look original. Money, money, money," Beth mocked. "Funny what happens to those sweet mid-Western liberals."

"Now look what's happening to Theo," Rose Ann answered. "What do you think?"

"I think you're gettin' catty, my sweet." The two of them were talking in conspiratorial tones, dropping their scarves and jackets on one of the couches that was becoming the impromptu repository of a pile of outer garments. They gratefully dropped themselves into easy chairs in the far corner of the space.

Rose Ann meant the big change in Theo's fortunes. He'd gone from couch surfing to landowner in a matter of weeks after his book was signed with a slick uptown publisher. He must have scored some advance. It was the talk of their gang, most of whom were only out of school a few years, and trying to cram art life into the time left over after marginal make-do jobs. Suddenly Theo was able to buy a whole top floor on Avenue C, a world away from Lois's ancient dumbbell walk-up on the same avenue. Rose Ann was thrilled to report that his new place was being converted from four former cold-water flats into a doublewide window-lined super crib. With the work still in progress Max had offered Theo his new place in Brooklyn for the book launch after-party.

It seemed, the two women realized, warming to their gossip vibes, something was happening now between Max and Theo's big sister Britz. She was some kind of scientist, friends had said. "She sure looks at home here," Beth grinned.

There was unexpected honking out on the street as a taxi disgorged four more people. There were rarely any cars let alone taxis on that street. The new arrivals trooped in along with a few other Vinegar Hill people who hadn't been at the Gotham Book Mart do. A printmaker, another painter, a young performance art hopeful. A furnace rumbled below as incomers admitted more January chill. Someone started up a stereo sending out soft piano music. Conversation definitely overwhelmed the music. Everyone was high on the excitement around Theo's book. An amazing surreal tale, with a percussive back beat. It was the holy grail of novelists, a genuinely avant-garde prose invention and a can't- put-it-down page-turner.

Britz, as tall, pale, and leggy as Theo, but less romantically featured, was bringing out bowls of hot-spiced beans, fresh veggies, hot tortillas, salsa. Her long brown hair was tied at the base of her neck with a thick twine cord. She had a butcher's apron over her t-shirt and well-worn jeans, and dangling crystal earrings that echoed the light in her hazel eyes. As Max dispensed wines and beer at the far end of the counter, people armed with food and drink began collapsing onto the several sagging sofas and easy chairs. There was a large kitchen table with chairs near the counter but at this point in the party, people wanted fluidity.

"I'll never get out of here," Rose Ann complained, struggling to rise. Thanks to her ample thighs her plump frame had been sucked down into a too-soft overstuffed chair.

Beth's tart reply was cut off by the growing volume of an altercation among Theo and two of the other guests. One had come in the taxi, the other was Burton MacIllerny, who lived on the other side of the street in Vinegar Hill. The exchange was clearly hostile.

"Quit lying, Theo. I know where that book came from!" MacIllerny was a cliché of fey belligerence with his hands on his hips and his head projecting forward.

"What are you saying?" Theo sucked his lower lip.

"You know damn well what I'm saying. I've got a fuckin' photographic memory."

"I don't know what you're talking about, Burton!" Theo protested.

"You better listen to him," said the second man. "He's consulted lawyers and everything. "

"Eddy!" Burton called out to a skinny redhead who was gobbling tacos by the kitchen counter. "Come on over here. It's time for a lil reckoning ya know."

"I, I, I want you to leave, both of you. Eddy too," Theo stammered. "Britz!"

Her arms were around a large wooden salad bowl full of multi-colored chips. "What's all this?" she asked. Other partygoers quieted and some stopped almost mid-motion, frankly gaping. Above the yelling voices Aretha Franklin now soared out of the stereo.

"Your brother fucking stole that manuscript from Jimmie. You know who I'm talking about. James Nexfield. The day he died. For all we know, this creep pushed poor Jimmie down the cellar steps," Burton told the crowd.

"Oh for godsake, Nexfield didn't die in a fall. He choked on food," Max interceded, taking the salad bowl from Britz. "What's all this about? Lawyers? I mean it Burton, what the hell do you think you're pulling?"

"I've seen lawyers. Trouble is—and the creep knows it—there's no paper trail, nothing at all. There's nothing but my word. But I know. I read the first half. Jimmie showed me. I read it and I remember every single word. And word for damn word, that's what this creep has published as his own. Lawyer says I can't do anything." Burton gulped. "No standing. Just my word. My worth not worth much with my drug history. Not worth much without a goddamn shred of something.... But I *know*..." He choked.

He'd meant to threaten social retaliation, he'd intended to be forceful, to maintain a steady thoughtful voice that would stir a crowd reaction, something to start some retribution for the travesty that had drained his dead friend. Emotion and a pre-party line of cocaine drove him up the hill. His voice broke into a ragged high register, his speech became babble, and it was hard for him to keep breathing. In frustration, Burton grabbed Theo's jacket lapels and shook him so hard his feet left the ground. Theo, in tears, sputtered, "no, NO!"

"Stop it," Britz screamed.

"It's not the end of this," Burton panted, spittle flying from the corners of his mouth. He hadn't loosened his hold on Theo's jacket, and the jacket back was splitting with a sound not unlike another cry. "This is a small world and I'm telling *everybody*. You stole that book, you filthy fucker!"

"Put him down," Max bellowed. "And leave my house. You too, Eddy."

"Everybody's fuckin' gonna know!" Burton promised. "Come my house," he added incoherently, as the guy from the taxi retrieved his overcoat and the three made their way out the door, through the gate, and across the cobbles to the corner house that Burton and Eddy shared. Max's guests were still gaping as Britz led the weeping Theo into a back bedroom. Max offered everyone refills and someone brilliant put a quiet Mozart violin concerto on the stereo.

§

"So how much is true," Max asked. Theo, Britz, and he were at the table. There was a fresh pot of coffee Max had made as the last guest left. Theo's face was mottled from crying but his nose had stopped running.

"None," said Britz, "none!" Her delicate mouth was trembling.

"Theo?" Max pressed.

Silence.

"Theo!" It was almost like a line of song from Britz.

"It was so good," Theo whispered after a long pause.

"Theo" she sang-said again.

"It was lying on the stairs, pages. I couldn't stop reading. I couldn't..."

"Good God," Max said at last.

"Now what do we do?" Britz asked Max.

Tears were rolling down Theo's cheeks again. Britz looked gut-shot.

The options are pretty stark, Max calculated. Confession, self-exposure? The publishing company would sue. They'd certainly have cause. Theo had surely signed more than a dozen documents attesting to his authorship. This

14

was no mistake. It was criminal fraud. Theo could be looking at jail if he couldn't pay the publisher for damages. At the very minimum the advance would have to be returned and Theo has already spent most of it. Britz had mentioned that Theo had borrowed more, on the strength of his large advance and the reading tours and college lecture stints his publisher was contracting. Renovating the apartment he'd bought on the Lower East Side was drinking money. It would all crash around him. Max ran his hands through his hair, his mind machine-gunning through possibilities.

So who else knows? How bad is bad? Burton has nothing to support his claim. If anyone else recognized James's text, they were not very likely. . .well, Max assured himself . . . someone with hard evidence would have spoken up by now what with all the pre-publication coverage. An excerpt had run in *The Atlantic*, a profile with a photo in *The Village Voice*. *The New Yorker* was sending someone to interview him. Hell, even gossip columnists had written about the book. An image of Liz Smith rose in Max's mind like a bad moon in a dirty sky.

He leaned over to Britz, and stroked her hair.

"Burton won't get anywhere," he announced, pouring himself more coffee.

"The capacity to blunder slightly is the real marvel of DNA. Without this special attribute, we would still be anaerobic bacteria and there would be no music."
—Lewis Thomas, M.D.

DAMAGE CONTROLS

Britz stayed in Sunday. Slept most of the day. She stayed in Monday too, calling the Dawson Center lab where she worked with a vague excuse about an earache. Monday, she and Max did post-party housework together, not talking about anything but clean-up things: how well the old floors were taking to mopping with Murphy oil, what to do with studio garbage, rags tainted with turps, polymer pastes, used up paint tubes. Monday afternoon Max went into his studio and she could hear charcoal hard against paper as he did sketch after sketch. They must have been violent. She didn't phone Theo, and he didn't call her either. Max was waiting for her to talk she guessed, and what was there to say? How could Theo do this? The question was relentless.

By Tuesday she had pulled herself together enough to manage the subway into Manhattan. Uptown. Face the people and place where she worked as a lab tech. The Dawson Center was an enormous cancer research facility combined with a hospital. Comprehensive cancer center, it was dubbed. Abundantly financed by wealthy donors and the federal government's war on cancer, it filled an entire block. The hospital part faced the opposite side of the block the research labs occupied, so there was no need to confront the tense and terrified people who pooled around the flossy hospital doorway and populated the wide waiting areas just inside.

The day was clear and crisp, with a stunningly blue winter sky. Britz breathed in some calm to fortify herself as she neared the lab doorway. The brightness darkened immediately as she entered the stark tiled hallway with yellow light bulbs and a complement of bored security guards. She was late. It was already after 11:30.

Two lab workers were hunched over a transistor radio when she made her quiet entrance. In her head she had been playing out a workable excuse for lateness following her absence but there was no need. The two men had no interest in it.

"The *Challenger* just blew up," Shahid said. His pale brown face was shocked, frightened. He was a medical research fellow, doing a two-year plunge into lab work following his M.D. in hope of qualifying as a research-physician. Shahid was intensely conscious of the protocols he needed to follow to procure advancement but blissfully unaware of the general forbearance if not open contempt of the veteran techs. They were constantly on the lookout for Shahid's technical slip-ups.

The usually glum Karl Ziek betrayed just a hint of satisfaction at the news. Karl was a bigger cheese, a senior post-doc researcher with a full fellowship that paid his salary and gave him a leg up for an academic research career. He filled Britz in, leaning his beefy frame over the table holding the transistor. "No one knows what happened, but za crew's kaput. Not two minutes after lift off. What a screw up. Heads gonna roll down in Florida."

Unlike Shahid, whose English was meticulous and correct, Karl spoke with a heavy Czech accent, matching his heavy sense of himself as an outsider and an exile.

"Are they really all dead?" Britz asked.

"Fireball. Not a chance."

"GOD DAMNIT, we getting work done today or what?" Ji-yoo was shrill. "We've got all these plates for the centrifuge needing a check. Something wrong with those elutriation rotors. I'm getting error message. If we have to call support we're gonna waste a day! And what with you?" she looked sharply up at Britz from under her sleek black bangs.

It wasn't a question of being believed. Getting sick was not an option for Ji-yoo. She'd probably keep working with two broken legs, Britz thought. Everyone else is upset, but not little Miss Nose to the Grindstone. Best team manager on the seventh floor.

The flow of news reports didn't stop, nor did the conversations. In place of the usual sporadic joking, questions swirled among the techs and grad students. Winston Stiles, the other top post-doc, was stunned. His long well-toned torso was almost doubled over in disbelief. Who had screwed up? What had failed? Why hadn't NASA aborted the mission? There had been trouble for days, and just before the weekend a snap freeze ravaged coastal Florida, he reported. That should have signaled some repeat testing, right? Another recheck? Other lab staff jabbered on and on, with Shahid urgently defending the NASA officials, Karl belittling them, and Winston peppering the air with logical hypotheses.

"Is all for show, all Cole War propaganda!" Karl

roared. "Juss wait. There's be one big cover story. Big dust in the air! You Americans. Always hurry, hurry, hurry. Always everything so cool. Everything sweet. Always no problem!"

In the lab, it was hard to know who the "you Americans" were. The place was staffed with an international collection of humans. Winston was the only white US-born suburb-raised person among them.

Britz recoiled at Karl's obvious delight at the way lethal world events were supporting his preferred position.

"Americans get things done! We'd all be like your precious Czech-o-Slovak-Keeah if we sat on our cynical cans." Shahid broke in, clearly undeterred by Karl. Shahid customarily wore spotless t-shirts adorned with eagles or American flags while most of the lab workers, regardless of their place in the hierarchy, showed up in well-used shirts with double entendre puns or colorful rock 'n roll imagery. Britz and Ji-yoo were the only women. They both favored the loose hospital issue scrubs available in the nurses' dressing rooms. They came in a bright turquoise with the institute's name embroidered in white and forest green. Britz wondered idly if Shahid had ever travelled beyond the protective cocoon of universities and research labs to encounter the reactions his Pakistani heritage might evoke in some of his beloved Americans.

The arguments began turning on ethics. From the possible damage to science funding, they went on to dissect the obvious unwillingness to report bad news. The difficulty inherent in supporting unwelcome facts.

"And personal ambitions," asserted Winston. His t-shirt sported a grinning gap-toothed Alfred E. Newman with Newman's classic "What me worry?" slogan in a speech balloon.

The possibility of official lies plus the death of all seven astronauts, including the young schoolteacher who was indeed on board for Cold War propaganda purposes, was making Britz's stomach churn. Integrity, she was thinking, which is so essential to sound science, is in daily conflict with institutional hierarchies. But how could Theo of all people have stolen! That morning she and Max had broken silence or Max had.

Cover up, cover up, cover up was the plan he advocated. Britz had to admit to herself and to Max that this was not the first time in her life that she had had to lie. But the need for initial cover up spiraled from possibility to possibility. Was anybody else involved in Theo's theft?

"Britz, your silence isn't the best idea," Max had counseled. "You need to call Dora and Lois and Bill and let them tell you what they think. You don't want to let Burt MacIllerny get ahead of you on this. And you don't want to squash him with a legal threat. That would just bring doubt and more publicity. Right now gossip is your *friend*. Reassure your friends first. Plus Theo should tell his agent and his editor all about the blowup at the party. Right away. Look," he said to her expressionless face, "it's clearly just a jealousy thing. And that's all. Happens all the time. Come on, Britz, you've gotta do it and get Theo to do it."

§

The police investigation into James' death a year ago had been difficult enough, Britz remembered. A lot of piercing questions had been fired at Theo. The forensic team was certain the dirt floor at the foot of the stairs had been disturbed, and Theo couldn't account for it no matter how they pummeled him. The questioning had become wider and more sinister. Where were the contents of the empty box? Exactly how long had Theo been there? Why so long? The pattern of injuries left open a central issue. Did James fall or was he pushed?

Then the issue ended quietly when the official medical examiner's report declared death by choking on food. A gob of meat was found lodged in the man's windpipe, a common enough disaster despite widespread knowledge of the Heimlich maneuver. Many choking victims do just what Mr. Nexfield did, someone in the ME office commented. Retreat to a private place.

Theo's paralysis was then pronounced understandable, even common. His friends were satisfied. The cops were satisfied. Friends and former students of James Nexfield moved on. As for his family, James had been estranged from them for years. They were somewhere in the Deep South and nobody turned up to mourn or manage or even inquire about an insurance policy death benefit. His friends knew his parents had denounced him, a blot on the family honor. And James had returned their insult with an icy and final cut-off.

To their credit, New School administrators stepped in to arrange a burial. James had been teaching there eleven years. They held a brief remembrance meeting in one of the lecture halls, then emptied and turned over his office. The landlord cleared out his apartment and the infamous basement study. All contents disposed of. Case closed.

Tight enough? That was something to consider.

Had James ever published anything that might connect his work to Theo's book? Britz knew MacIllerny would look. Yes, she'd talk to Theo right after work.

> "As we were driving home tonight we saw someone we knew walking a dog. A second later we remembered this person doesn't have dog. Clearly the person we saw walking the dog was not the person we thought. Instead it was another person we knew who does have a dog."
>
> —Anonymous

WATERFRONT WALKING PARTY

Britz had left for work way too late for Max to follow his usual morning routine. He liked to start the day early by meeting up with Gray, a neighbor dog owner and going with him on his dawn rounds. They kept a lively pace and rarely spoke about anything beyond dog endearments and gossip about other dogs. Whatever the weather, it was bracing to trot through the waterfront streets at dawn. Harbor water scented the air even though access to the river itself was for the most part blocked. The variations in light and weather fascinated Max every day. The rhythms primed him for his work. He'd get back to his building in time for a coffee with Britz, see her off and be ready for the studio.

He didn't want a dog of his own though it might have been easy to acquire one. Eight years had elapsed since the city passed the Canine Waste law, better known as the "Poop Scooper" rule, requiring dog walkers to remove droppings or risk fines. As soon as the law passed, people drove to the nearly deserted Brooklyn waterfront in the hours between dusk and dawn and left dogs on the street. It took months for Vinegar Hill to recover from a flood of roaming strays. Hard to fathom, impossible to excuse, but there it was, Max thought with disgust when he heard the tale. People too fine to deal with their own pet's shit, too cheap, too irresponsible. Even now, with the law mostly honored, and the streets cleaner because of it, people still used the waterfront to dump unwanted animals now and then. Occasionally a fine expensive breed would be among them. The lost dogs would deteriorate visibly and slowly disappear. By death or by dognapping. This was not a neighborhood where people were likely to phone Animal Control about a stray.

Eight months ago Gray had taken up with a huge light brown finely bred Greyhound, skittish, thin, and worm-infested.

"He took up with me," Gray pointed out. "Started following me. Sat outside right on my door! What could I do?" Because Britz had stopped on a corner for this speech, the animal eagerly circled Gray's legs, lithe muscles working under a now a shiny fawn-colored coat. The dog looked up adoringly, moist black nose and unusual sparkling eyes as gray as Gray's name. The change in Gray was just as dramatic, and he knew it.

"You know I had the shakes, Britz. Couldn't stop. I was pretty close to cashing out. Fuck all. But I had . . .well, I *had* to. Fall weather was starting and I could tell he wasn't gonna make it without care. Not just the food, he needed everything! Right Constable? Right g'boy?" Gray pounded the dog's wide rib cage and fondled the softly folded ears.

Eight months with outdoor walking dawn and twilight, and of having a loving creature craving attention, a big warm dog body lying on his bed at night—and Grey too was ten pounds heavier and seemingly inches taller. Somewhere along his first weeks with Constable, he'd started AA meetings. "Couldn't be passed out when he needed a walk," he almost apologized. Now he no longer goes down the street with arms crossed over his chest, furtively hunched over. Instead of temping when he was able to work at all, a sober Grey had scored a full time job this past summer. Something in computers. Apparently it paid very well. "Gotta pay those vet bills," he joked. "Besides, I seem to have a real knack for coding. It just comes. Besides," again apologizing for his recovery, "ya know he needs me," prompting one of Britz's dazzling smiles.

Today, without Gray or Constable, Max avoided the usual routes around Dumbo. Instead he circled the abandoned Navy Yard and followed Kent Avenue, exploring how close he could get to the East River's Wallabout Channel. He longed for a way down to the water, water to cool his worry, but there was no access, no way that was not blocked by fencing, building deconstruction, and muddy no-man's lands. Max turned away from the multiple "Keep Out" signs and retraced his steps, mulling. The domestic affection between dog and man so fine and restorative for his friend Gray made unwanted thoughts swirl about him unpleasantly. He had lived over ten years with Betsy and their breakup had been raw.

I once found Betsy's practical instincts almost magical, he mused, now I think those very instincts led her to hook up with that cheap bastard Alex. All he wants out of pottery is a bucket of cash. Betsy thought he was *practical*. Fuckin' nuts. Single minded chase for loot's more like it. So goodbye Betsy with her simple ideas of goodness.

She's up to her neck now in a money game with Alex. Loving it I bet. Good riddance, he steamed, remembering one particularly bitter screaming fight. But then he had to cut back and ruefully consider his own situation. A huge switch in his methods and materials had plunged him into an art world swirl: His current work was deemed "neo-expressionist" "new realism" "new surrealism"— whatever various critics wanted to tag it with now that AbEx was "so over."

The new work he'd begun brimmed with story, characters, transformations, and garnered so much excitement among museums and gallery dealers that he fled Soho. When he found deserted Vinegar Hill he dove in. What a relief to be where "no one" lived, to walk streets of no galleries, boutiques, chic restaurants. No tourists. No wannabees. No "scene." He was seeking control, not abdication. And it had been working. He'd met Britz. He'd met Britz and he'd been feeling a new opening. They could cross over between science and art. They each had ideas and experiences new to the other. Life could be new. New until now.

What was Theo's revelation going to do to her? How was she going to reconcile her life-long devotion to him and her bright silver streak of ethics? Theft. Forgery! By her beloved brother? And what was he, Max, going to do with Britz? She was almost fifteen years younger than he. What was he *doing* falling in love with her? As if he could master the way his physical thirst had twisted around his fascination with the way her intellect clicked like a fine machine. The passion about research and its rigors she exposed when she explained the lab's projects to him. Or when she brought home a scientific journal to explain why reported results were not all that exciting. Of course she had to be beautiful too. The fine bones in her face. The slender neck any ballet dancer would covet. Of course this line of thought was a cheap out too, wasn't it? He had had choices and he'd made them. He could undo them too. He gritted his teeth. If he had to he could.

> "To distinguish such a mariner from those who mere-
> ly...run aloft, furl sails, haul ropes, and stand at the
> wheel, they say he is 'a sailor man;' which means that
> he not only knows how to reef a topsail but is an artist
> in the rigging."
>
> —Herman Melville

RIGGING IS A VERB

"Miller wants to see you," Karl announced.

It was not quite five yet, and the lab normally buzzed on till six, six-thirty or later, but Britz was already closing down her bench work. The *Challenger* disaster and the need to get Theo's cooperation batted forth and back in her mind like an evil game of badminton, wrecking her concentration and making her hands shake when they definitely shouldn't. She hated fucking up materials; she hated not being fully capable of precision.

"Miller?" She sounded disoriented, downright demented Karl was thinking, assessing her expression.

"Dr. Judah Miller, M.D., Ph.D., awarded the Lasker Prize Miller, you don't know who you work for?"

"Oh good lord," Britz said, gathering a clipboard and pen, and pushing flyaway hair back from her face.

Dr. Miller was hunched over a large printout when she knocked and opened the door to his private office.

"Yah, yah, Ms. Gondelieve, ah, I mean Ms. Henneberg, I need some work here."

The sound of her actual first name gave Britz another lurch. Only her parents ever called her "Gondelieve." She stood at attention waiting.

"There's something with these data, maybe how they were entered, something, something off." He went on running a pencil, eraser side down, along spread sheet columns in the printout. Then with deliberation he carefully folded the several large pages together so they would fit in a large yellow clasp envelope.

"I want you to back check all of this. And do it at home. It's not helpful to have a lot questions coming in right now. " He was still looking down, fumbling with the little metal fastening clasp. "I'll inform Ms. Yoo you're on assignment."

He held out the envelope for her.

"By Friday. Sooner if you can." He finally looked up, nailing her through his rimless glasses with hard grey-blue eyes. "You won't discuss this except with me. Thank you."

She'd been dismissed. She would have been mystified if she had not been so preoccupied. As it was, she realized with some annoyance that she'd have to check through all the documents in the envelope to copy supporting data from the central file onto floppy disks for use in her computer at home. Plus she'd have to broach Dr. Miller's iron-faced administrator to sign for permission to copy files. A time-consuming pile-up of chores.

She was right. It was well past six thirty before she could leave. Ji-yoo was the only one left, apparently stacking plates in the autoclave to be sterile for the next day's work. They didn't speak. The radio was off, mercifully.

§

The spreadsheets were all related to recent clinical trial outcomes testing the effectiveness of a new treatment for stroke. Lab work on the active ingredient in the drug had been done in Miller's lab perhaps three years before Britz had begun working there. Maybe seven, eight years ago? The thought did ping at her: why had she been asked to do this review when she'd never been involved in any of the pre-clinical studies, let alone the clinical ones, the tests with actual stroke patients. Surely someone more familiar with this project?

On the other hand, data is data, and she was greatly relieved to be able to work on a quiet puzzle in the peacefulness of Max's Vinegar Hill hideaway. She would need quite a bit of time for talking to people about Theo's scene with Burton. Easier to do that if she had privacy and could juggle her hours as she saw fit. Was that awful dust-up only last Saturday night?

Her backpack pulled at her shoulders as she trudged toward the subway through the cold. She'd taken some binders from the pharmaceutical firm supplying the test meds and the weight cut into her collarbones. I could be a serf lugging firewood in a Breughel painting. Godelieve! Martyred saint of Bruges. Theodore, just simple Greek, the gift of God. It makes me shiver, the way our parents were always thinking. They were cult-fanatics, the pair of them. Thank you, thank you Theo for coming up with a better name for me. The image of little two-year-old Theo earnestly spitting out "Britz" was hugely calming. They had needed each other so much.

30

"Lisa gave me a plant with lovely white flowers, brought down from her house in Piermont. Charming. It reverted to purple the very next year and invaded. Now, after a very modest flowering in May, these violets launch giant stubborn leaves everywhere . . . .violent and marauding, not shy at all. Beloved of slugs. Slugs eat them but not nearly enough. Now both are everywhere!"

—Martha King, Garden Plagues,
unpublished prose-poem

WHAT HAPPENS TO PHONE CALLS

"Hey Dora, j'ah know that guy from across the street? Burt, Burton? That was quite a story he sprang on us!" Britz was sprawled on one of Max's sofas with the telephone balanced on her belly. Dora was at work in the Welfare Office, but it turned out she welcomed the break. Britz could hear her kick the door to her small office shut.

"He's an odd bird, Britz."

"How do you know him?"

"I don't really, I just know of him. My friend Chris, you know him, he has that little bookshop on 7th Street? This guy Burton came to see him about selling a bunch of letters from Aaron Copland. Love letters to a boy violin prodigy. Steamy stuff. Chris wanted to know if I knew him. He thought the letters were real but he sure didn't trust that this Burton hadn't stolen them from someone."

"I didn't know Copland was gay."

"Oh come on, Britz."

"What could you do for him?"

"Chris? Nothing really. Well I suppose I could have checked to see if Burton was in our system anywhere. We do have a lot of info, links to D.A.'s and stuff like that. But I just told Chris stay clear of him. I was kind of shocked when he walked into Max's place."

"He lives just across the street."

Dora withdrew into circumspect silence.

"So what do you think?" Britz pressed.

"Craziness."

That was all. Dora switched the conversation to talk about Max. To pin Britz down about the relationship, about what she was thinking and whether this was a serious thing or not.

"Come on, Britz. Give!"

"Oh Dora, I'm just having fun," Britz lied.

"Funny how I don't believe you. But you'll tell me when you tell me," she compromised, ending the phone call on a soft note.

Dora had been a punk performance artist in her earlier life and had managed to have three children along with her spot performance gigs—first twin girls and then a little boy, plus a parade of men friends, none of whom were at all interested in being a parent. Britz never figured out why Dora was so interested, but being a parent turned out to be an enormous thing for her. She kept her kids fed and clean and centered while she maneuvered her way through the city's welfare system, first collecting under two different names and never getting caught. Then she got support to finish undergraduate work, acquired a position in the department, and began her rise.

Along the way she landed an apartment in subsidized

housing and fostered a homeless teenager, who proved wonderfully adept at childcare. By the time her foster kid had finished college Dora was a senior counselor and halfway to her own Ed.D. The wildly colored hair, the nose rings and tattoos were ditched or hidden under makeup. Dora was happy to apply her smarts and curiously belligerent empathy to handling hapless clients and gormless bureaucrats alike. Their contrast and similarities greatly appealed to her sense of humor. And they in turn were often taken off balance by her coarse manners, abrupt language and surprising erudition. Britz predicted she'd have a six-figure salary and a senior title to go with it before her own three kids were out of college.

After hanging up Britz realized she hadn't completed her mission: she'd said nothing to Dora to exonerate Theo and done nothing to caution her against spreading gossip.

It wouldn't have done any good anyway, she consoled herself. Still she felt she could trust Dora not to keep too much from her. She had a mellow friendship with Dora and Dora and Theo had even longer links to each other.

The next phone call was not as reassuring. Lois. She was at home, working. She too had links with Theo, years of friendship, hours of talk. Not really mother and son stuff, but Theo's respect for powerful and contrary women kept them connected. Funny, Britz was thinking, how consistently comfortable Theo was with older people, especially women. As for Lois, her step was still as firm it had been in her twenties when she powered through union vigils and war protests. These days she's hiking up five flights to her rent-controlled apartment, and navigating around the boarded up store fronts and gutted vacant lots pocking the far east edge of the Lower East Side. Increasingly she spends hours chasing down copyediting and fact checking jobs for a shrinking roster of edgy publications. She's not an easy sell for anyone on anything.

"Listen, Britz, I'm hearing a lot of echoes here," Lois said, her suspicion well-honed by her association with Dr. Reich. "You know how taken Theo was with James Nexfield. I remember how he couldn't stop talking about Nexfield's class. About his writing. About how important his writing was. After he died, that talk stopped cold."

"Hey, he was devastated," Britz asserted. "But really I saw that as a kind of spark. That was when he started working every day. Writing every day I mean. He was on fire."

"Be honest with me. Doesn't that make you just a little uncomfortable?"

"Theo would never, *never*..."

"Don't screech at me, woman. I know you love him."

"It's more than love. Lois! I've known him since he was born. I *know* him. I know him like nobody else does." She was close to tears with the knowledge that she'd lost control and was actually confirming Lois's suspicions.

Sure enough, Lois switched from cynical interrogator to soothing big sister, and ended the call by assuring Britz how fond of Theo she'd been for years.

"Theo stood by me when I was all in. You know that, Britz."

Lois meant by that she'd be 'on his side' without being convinced of his innocence.

"It's gonna be okay, kid," she concluded.

Not exactly the outcome Britz hoped for. She pushed

the phone back onto a side table, got off the couch, launched her computer, and began reviewing clinical trial data.

§

Two hours later she'd hit a wall. She got a cup of coffee, opened the front door for a quick gulp of wintry air, and started over from the beginning. Then Max came in from his studio and wanted lunch. Deeply preoccupied, she helped him on half power. They made tuna fish sandwiches together while she hardly noticed the care he was taking not to disturb her.

There was a dizzying array of tests to determine the level of post-stroke recovery but very little to pin down the timing issues. What was "early" exactly? When did the critical first three-hour window for effective treatment really begin? How did they select matching groups of patients for a double-blind study? The bigger the number of subjects the more likely the results will be statistically valid. Research design 101, she thought. But that wasn't quite it.

She loved the term "double-blind" conjuring for her all the possible ways a person could be blind, even though she knew it was science-ese for clinical trials where neither the patients or any of the healthcare professionals know who is in which group There are always built-in precautions, sometimes very elaborate ones, to keep secret who got the active test treatment, who got a lookalike sugar pill or a sham intervention and who got no treatment at all. Everyone is "unblinded" only when the trial is over.

Phlegm: the thick viscous substance secreted by the mucous membranes of the respiratory passages, especially when produced in excessive or abnormal quantities. ...In medieval science and medicine one of the four bodily humors, believed to be associated with a calm, stolid, or apathetic temperament.

—*Lexico.com*

WHO KNOWS ENOUGH?

It was Thursday morning already and Dr. Miller wanted her report Friday. Plus Theo had not called his agent or his editor.

"Don't worry, Britz. I'll get to it. I promise," was all she could get out of Theo.

She flinched hearing this over the phone. Didn't he get it? Maybe Max should talk to him. But Max would tell her *she's* the perfect messenger, she's the one who'd have Theo's confidence. Instead of being distraught and possibly more unglued, Theo had apparently bounced into doing the next things in his life without a backward glance at the threats from Burton MacIllerny. "Don't worry, don't worry. I'm fine," was his reply. Thursday the *New Yorker* reporter was coming! He did a poor job of disguising how thrilled he was.

Damn, Britz thought. That interview was sure to use up all his time that day. Well, Friday, then. Would he make the calls he promised then?

And I just don't know enough, her sticky internal dialog continued. Burton's gonna find something wrong.

Wrong. There's something wrong in the way the clinical studies measured stroke damage and the time of first treatment. The line between "early" and "very early" is arbitrary, meaningless, she scribbled in her notes. Did that three-hour window begin with the first appearance of a stroke symptom? Common sense says one person might have had stroke symptoms hours, even a day, before arriving at a hospital or stroke center, while another person with similar disease is under medical care within two or three hours. So the stats had begun to look off. Too many numbers were almost identical. Is there fraud here? The test groups look beautifully balanced, the studies are "elegant"—but, but, but. No answer, no ending, she concluded angrily.

"Don't worry so, Britz. I'll get to it," Theo had said.

"Don't worry so Britz. Why are you thinking the treated patients had milder strokes in the first place?" Britz asked herself.

She had promised Miller not to discuss the assignment he'd given her but she phoned the lab and asked for Shahid.

"Gota minute?" She made herself sound cheerful and calm. "I need a little background. Didn't you tell me you loved your neurology rotation? Can you catch me up on how stroke damage data are normally collected? Early on I mean. Day one?"

He was flustered and then both puzzled and flattered. He had an M.D. and she didn't. He'd had experience with sick people, not just aberrant mice or lab managed cells. He plunged into some stroke basics as he would have recited them to an attending physician on hospital rounds.

Then he stopped, his confusion and suspicion mounting. She had to give him more.

After a deep breath, Britz told him Dr. Miller had some worries about the integrity of some data and she was doing deep background for him. She'd imagined Shahid would continue being flattered at being in on this. Instead he erupted.

"What do you think you're doing!" He was almost screaming at her, a complete breach of his normal behavior. "You better fix that!" he shrilled. "You're not going to show him any errors. You are *not*!"

"Shahid! This is not for you to say. Listen. Listen to me. I want you to meet me tomorrow morning at eight sharp. In the Eat Well deli on the uptown corner, not our cafeteria. I'll show you exactly where I am. I need your cooperation on this. I mean it!"

As she hung up, she was sure she heard him hiss, "Bitch."

God, what have I done...what have I stepped into? These drug development schemes mean a great deal of money to many powerful people. Stroke! Suppose this data helps get the new med cleared as a first line treatment? That'd be hundreds of thousands of patients using it every year. What damage could it do? And if it really works—what a payoff! Saving brains, saving useable lives. It flicked through her mind like a collage: donor money, promotions, job offers . . . Nobel prize!

Britz took a deep breath and dialed Bill's home number. She got his answering machine. "Just wondering what you think about that crazy outburst from MacIllerny. Catch me later. I'm at Max's," she dutifully recorded, and then listened to a record saying, "To edit your message, press one; to delete your message, press two; to send your message, please hang up." It was repeated three or four times before Britz returned the receiver to its cradle.

It had been dark for a long time when the phone rang again. She'd been chopping celery for a salad and carefully keeping her worries at bay. Max was in the shower, cooling down and cleaning up from his day's work. She'd made a cassoulet and sweet spicy smells from the oven had begun to permeate the kitchen. What now? To her relief the caller was Shahid. Then he said he wanted to meet her tonight, he had an early appointment on Friday, and couldn't see her then. He sounded urgent but much more polite. He apologized for shouting. He apologized for telephoning in her private time. But would ten o'clock tonight be okay? To give him time to prepare for the next day. He wanted directions to the Vinegar Hill neighborhood. He'd come to her he said.

She thought a minute before she told him she'd meet him in the only possible impersonal place: four blocks up Hudson Avenue was an Italian lunch counter restaurant. She and Max were very aware of the gleaming pimpmobiles that habitually pulled up in front around noon. Gaudily dressed men, mostly black, emerged from these cars and strolled in and exited in a few minutes. She'd been in the place late one morning while Max was getting lasagna take-out and seen a man at the back table with a mound of cash bigger than a softball in his left hand, from which he peeled three one-hundred dollar bills, folded them with his right hand, and handed them across the table to another man. Max had given her a soft shove, to stop her staring.

We never wanted to leave home. . . . Was there a war?
. . . . Everything is normal, very normal.
—*Lost, Lost, Lost*, a film diary by Jonas Mekas, 1976

MISSING

Max woke with a start. He was in an easy chair, a copy of *Mother Jones* on the floor between his feet.

"Hey Britz."

No answer.

"Britz!" somewhat louder.

What the hell? Supper had been delicious and filling. He'd gone back into his studio to push his new painting further and after a few hours, nearly dropping with fatigue, he'd stumbled out and plopped into one of the big chairs. Where was Britz he'd wondered, idly picking up a magazine and starting one of those infernal long *Mother Jones* investigation pieces. Cod fish, the changes brought by industrialized fishing, corporate evasion of traditions, possible threat to world food supply if current practices were not reined in. . . . Hey, where the hell is Britz!

He remembered fuzzily she'd put her head into the studio and said she needed a bit of air. Her Navy pea jacket was missing, and her handbag. He snapped on an outside light. Checked the time. Not quite eleven, not so late really, but where would she have gone? He should have said something. Asked her why the hell she wanted to go out.

Max stomped into the kitchen area, shoved up his sleeves and began clean up. KP it was called when he was a boy. Kitchen Patrol. Kitchen Police? Must have been some army term, he thought. He couldn't think why "KP" occurred to him. He tried not to think the word "police" as unbidden anxiety began to build.

At 11:30 he phoned Theo. The call alarmed him. He hadn't heard from Britz since early that morning and he hadn't spoken to his agent or his editor as she'd asked. He hoped she wouldn't be mad. He'd had an amazing interview with the *New Yorker* woman. He'd do the calls tomorrow. Friday. "Tell her!" Theo urged.

Max phoned Gray. He would have done his evening dog walk much earlier that evening but had he seen her? No. Not tonight.

He pulled on a jacket and went out to the street. Lights were on in Burton and Eddy's place opposite. She wouldn't have gone there, would she? After pacing a bit he rapped on their door. Burton was icy when he saw Max.

"Of course NOT, " he said, slamming the door.

It was cold and dark elsewhere on the street. A waning crescent moon was scudded over by clouds and the antiquated streetlight barely cut the gloom. Who else? Where else?

Max didn't want to stray far from his house as of course she'd be back and if he weren't there when she came in the two of them were all too likely start one of those awful round and rounds, missing each other at corner after corner. Funny in the movies. Ha. Ha. He did the sensible thing: went back inside, turned on more lights, and poured himself a stiff drink.

The magazine held no further interest for him. Johnny Carson. Two more drinks, the "Late Show's" sign-off, and his temper was flaring. On "The Tomorrow Show" Tom

Snyder was smoking a cigarette right on camera. "BRITZ!" he bellowed out of the front door. "God damn it!"

He made himself rein in curses and tried to stop the clanging "Britz, Britz, Britz" refrain in his head. He found a movie channel with a 1950's western. When he woke up again, the test pattern was running and it was way after three. Should he call hospitals, the police, her friends? Goddamn it no. Did the difference in their ages really mean he should get a grip and end the thing between them? He stripped and threw himself into bed. He woke up at 4:30, at 4:55, at 5:25, finally it was six a.m.

He scribbled big black letters on a large piece of drawing paper: "Britz! Stay put here. I've gone to look for you but I'll be back. STAY put!! MAX." He propped it upright in the sink, took money and a credit card, and went out for a serious search.

§

Midafternoon Friday he went to the police station over on Gold Street. She hadn't been missing 24 hours, he was told. She was an adult, he was told. Missing people turn up, he was told. We can't file a formal report for 24 hours, he was told. Are you her next of kin? Remember, anyone 18 or over without a history of mental disability has the right to keep their location private. We don't really know if she is missing. She may be acting on her own free will. Sorry fella, being missing from a boyfriend is not a crime.

"Look, she took only a small handbag and her pea jacket," he explained with calm detail. "All her clothes and her credit cards are at my place. Her books, her papers.

Her jewelry box. If she'd wanted to leave, she'd have taken things, personal stuff. Her toothbrush! Damnit, her prescription sunglasses are sitting on a shelf in the kitchen."

"Have you checked local hospitals?" the desk cop used a somewhat kinder tone. Max had done that in the morning. "Have you checked where she lived before moving in with you?" She'd moved most of her stuff to Vinegar Hill three months ago, but, Max remembered, her lease wasn't up till the end of April and she hadn't relinquished the keys. Late that afternoon he found them, took a train to Second Avenue, but there was no sign of her at her old apartment. He knocked on a few doors on her old floor and another by the front entrance. No one had seen anything of her.

No one at her lab had heard anything since the Tuesday when she'd come in for work. Britz was "on assignment" and this was clearly not the lab manager's problem she let him know though she did agree to call Max if she heard from her. She was a very business-like young Asian and clearly annoyed at being asked something not on her job description late on a Friday afternoon.

Britz's friends were far more alarmed than anyone at the lab. Dora offered help with more phone calls. Max gave her a list of phone numbers from Britz's address book. Theo was enlisting some of his friends for a sweep of Lower East Side hangouts—and at midnight he phoned Max, clearly stoned, asking if he could come over. Max said yes. Earlier, Lois wanted to come over just to be with him and she had proved evenly focused on the checklist of things needed for the missing person report that the desk sergeant had handed him. Together they scoured up two good recent photographs—and made out lists: a description of everything she was wearing even her underwear. A description of her handbag, its contents. They listed her physical stats including scars (there were two), and her most recent previous address. Her next of kin is Theo who would be the legal or official recipient of information but Max as the person who filed the complaint would be the contact.

He walked Lois to the F Train and went home to brace himself for Theo. Dealing with him would take skill and patience.

> However novel it may appear, I shall venture the assertion that until women assume the place in society which good sense and good feeling alike assign to them, human improvement must advance but feebly.
>
> —Frances Wright, 1829

OFFICIALLY MISSING

After six Friday afternoon, Max got a call from Britz's lab. It was not the lab head, Dr. Miller, but Karl Ziek, the top post-doc. Max felt his replies to questions about her whereabouts were perfunctory to say the least. Ziek mainly wanted to know if Max had the papers Britz had taken home on Tuesday. He even asked if he could come on out to Brooklyn to pick them up.

"Absolutely not!" Max roared. "They belong to Britz and *she'll* bring them back."

"They're important," Karl pressed.

"Listen you insensitive turd, if she has a report she hasn't filed, that's her business. She doesn't have anything here but copies and you or your boss must know it. She couldn't have taken anything precious. She made copies of your lab's stuff on floppy disks. Unless you have news of *her*, don't fucking call me again!" He was shaking with the emotions he had been keeping in check since Thursday night.

"Can you believe the nerve of that shithead!" he stormed to Theo. "Unreal!"

§

Over the endless weekend, the posters Max had made with Britz's photograph were attached to lampposts and subway walls, taped up in building lobbies, in favorite bars in Soho and on the Lower East Side and in the few businesses along the streets of adjoining Dumbo. The posters used the police department's hot-line phone number to spare him and Theo the inevitable cranks and pranksters. A rally of friends helped with the posting.

And now what?

All through the weekend, the weather held steady, cold and clear. Max and Gray and Theo tramped carefully through the neighborhood's empty lots, through alleys and around buildings, poked dead weeds, tried locked doors. More friends phoned.

Finally on Monday her photo and description were on the official missing person bulletin issued by the police to all five boroughs, airports, and bus and train stations. They were sent "personal attention" to the Dawson Center where Britz worked, and with Theo's reluctant participation to police in the town where their parents lived. Theo was urged to contact his parents directly. Now! To the annoyance of the cops, Theo wasn't quite sure where Britz had gone to school or lived before she came to New York City. They had not been in touch from the time Britz left home, years before. They had connected only here in New York about five years ago.

Dr. Miller, Britz's boss, telephoned Max. He had just heard the news, he said. Max and Theo have his sincerest concern he said. He said the institute's public affairs

46

office could help especially as he felt it would be intrusive to have newspapers or television stations involved at this juncture. The P.A. director could fend them off if they should appear. Max agreed. Dr. Miller gave him her name and a pager number to call her. He also asked Theo to consult with the institute's security department just to be sure they had all relevant information. Finally he supplied both Max and Theo with his personal phone number for news the minute there was any.

And there it sat.

"What do we do now," Max asked Theo. "Go over everything again?"

Yes. No. Limbo.

§

A police search team arrived Monday mid-morning to re-ask all the same questions Max and Theo had asked before beginning their search of the neighborhood. Max provided some unwashed clothing for the police dogs and the keys to Britz's old apartment. The cops did not want either of them tagging along. There were six of them, with walkie-talkies and poles for prodding broken ground.

"Sometimes family members make it harder for folks to give us leads," one of the search team members said, sounding friendly. He was trying to gloss over the implication that one or both of them could be under suspicion.

It was almost two-thirty when Max put his phone ringer on mute. They could hear callers' leaving messages which was quite enough.

"We have to stop drinking coffee, Theo. We need to eat, okay?" Theo had gone wooden, sinking into himself.

"Are you going to call your parents?" Max asked, presenting two beer bottles and a plate of cold cut and rolls. "The cops in what's the town? New Harmony? They're gonna make a house call when they see that bulletin."

"Not too many cops in New Harmony," Theo whispered. "Intentional community. You know. Old time communes?"

"Don't you think they should hear from you first?" Max insisted.

"Maybe six hundred people there," Theo continued. "Total."

"Even so, cops from the next big town," Max said.

"Ever heard of Robert Owen, Fanny Wright?" he blurted. Max shook his head.

"Scottish socialists, 19th century? Real heroes to my folks. You think these things are new? Fanny Wright was promoting sex equality, votes for women, birth control, abortion on demand no questions asked, the whole package. She meant what she said. Anything less would not be true freedom. Plus she pushed not just freedom for slaves but reparations and education. Cause she knew they'd be sitting ducks without capital or literacy. This was in the eighteen forties, man. She did have some crazy idea that slaves in the South could work to purchase their freedom so the economy wouldn't be disrupted by sudden mass emancipation. You can bet that went over. You really never heard of her?" His excitement kept building:

"Later she started a commune in Tennessee to house and teach black people. That was after emancipation. Obviously that didn't work either. It didn't spread like they hoped. But the only thing she and Owen did wrong per my parents was *atheism*. Old Fanny said the idea of a god didn't make sense in our great universe, and oh boy do my folks believe we gotta have god. Capital G god. No sex, no nationality, no church. Just plain vanilla major big power God cause all us poor humans end up having to lean on it."

"So what do they do in New Harmony?" Max interrupted, mystified by this stream of information.

"Lead meditations in the hedge labyrinth. At least my mother does. Our dad works. Well I hope so. He's often not a long-term employee, you could say. Man they kept us on the run the whole time we were growing up. Nothing and nowhere was ever leading to spiritual perfection. Not fast enough. Not right enough. So off we'd go. Fast. Oh yeah, we had to fast too. Britz and I got taught to pray with breathing. If we weren't praying we weren't listening to nature. We... Max! Where has she gone? You don't know what I went through when Britz left home."

"Did she just disappear, like this?"

No answer.

"Theo, don't nod off on me! Did she disappear like this?"

"No. She had a plan. We were in Tennessee, at The Farm. All San Francisco people, The Farm. Not us. We weren't members. Britz got Bro Edward to help her get a job at a local restaurant. Told him she wanted to study midwifery and her parents had religious objections. That was almost true. He was great. Helped her get I.D. Got the restaurant folks to give her a room. Upstairs over the kitchen. She snuck me in to see it before she split. She told me *everything*. She didn't just go. It was a plan. She was gonna come get me as soon as she could. But they dragged me off to the Theosophists."

"Whoa. What's that?"

"Some other commune. It was all the way across the country. California. I can't remember the name of the town. I couldn't even get a message to her about where I was."

Theo drank a large glass of water without taking a breath.

"What the hell is a hedge labyrinth?" Max asked.

"I don't know who was more freaked when she left, them or me," Theo said. "They kept me locked in the house for days. It was *weird*. Then we upped stakes and took a bus across the country. Just the three of us. The only good thing was the Halcyon place.

"Shit, that's the name, Halcyon! In California. The group, the town. Halcyon's a big spread for Theosophists, they have a giant temple there. Temple of the People. And lots of houses. A lot of brainy people living there, composers, *poets*— all different. Not like The Farm. They got me into high school. I guess they kind of overwhelmed my folks about education. I got to go to a regular school. First time in my life I was around books that weren't spiritual or occult. I didn't really want too much to do with any of the people but man, did I ever *read*! Novels, poetry. And I got math and history and art—it was breaking my head open. I was there five years. All the time I loved it but I had no one if I wasn't reading. I had had Britz and where was Britz? Where *is* she, Max? Do you think she's gone there? Halcyon, California?"

Max spent the rest of the afternoon calling California directory assistance, and finally when it was still afternoon in California, connecting with the Halcyon commune's Guardian, "the fourth Guardian" he was informed. The community had been founded in 1903. He was invited to visit, to learn their history and mission and even to consider purchasing one of the vacant houses, but sincerely sorry, the Guardian was certain, no one has seen or heard from any Henneberg since the senior Hennebergs left the community about nine-ten years ago. The Guardian wanted Theo to be in touch. He wanted a lot of things that had nothing to do with finding Britz, here and now in New York City.

"So Theo, what the hell is a hedge labyrinth?" Max asked after sharing all the Halycon information. During the phone calls, Theo had been making a small braid of his hair, coming down the left side of his face in front of his ear. He finished it off with a small red rubber band and began another ramble. Theo couldn't talk without creating an essay. It started with description of a large circular puzzle built of bricks or mud or even better with small planted bushes. The bushes would grow into thick hedges and be clipped to make narrow pathways in between.

"People go walking around inside," he said. "There'd be a big circle with lots of dead-ends and backtracking, lovely design, and a turnaround at the very middle. Only one way out."

"Corn mazes?" Max interrupted. He'd seen tourist attractions out in the country in the fall, with pumpkins and cider for sale, mostly at pick-em yourself apple orchards.

"No, no. That's a real cheesy derivative. The labyrinth

idea predates ancient Egyptians. Traces of them can be found all over the world. The Minotaur was kept in one!" Theo pronounced as if that explained everything. "Do you think I should make another one?" he asked, showing Max the second long thin braid of pale brown hair he'd just finished.

"Wait a second. You think your parents are keeping some mythological half bull critter out there in fucking Indiana!'

It was the first time that day that Theo laughed. "No, no, no, Max. It's like a metaphor for human life. They use labyrinths for a walking meditation. You know, zone out, just go walking for hours and hours in and around and around again, learning to be lost, learning to trust that you can find the center. It's, it's a *practice*. They even have them painted on the floors of cathedrals in Europe. But these ones have hedges. One you're inside, you can't see anything but a few feet of pathway."

Suddenly Max knew: It's going to be like that. It's going to be like that for days and days. He walked around his place, but not in a circle, put on his suede jacket and went out. Theo had curled up to read. He'd found Vasari's *Lives of the Painters* in Max's studio and plunged himself into the Italian Renaissance.

Max retraced the steps of his very first search, again around and around, until he ended up at the end of Dock Street. Where are you. Where are you. He climbed over the cement highway barrier and out onto a stretch of rough rocks splashed by the East River. He stood there a while and suddenly began to howl across the dark water. He howled to the night sky, pierced by planes threading overhead toward the city's three airports. The river water sucked and moaned. Tide was going out leaving behind smelly black crevasses between the rocks. Max howled until he was exhausted enough to stop. Then he waited. When hot tears stopped running into his beard he turned uphill and walked back home.

It is a confusing path, hard to follow without a thread,
but, provided [you are] not devoured at the midpoint,
it leads surely, despite twists and turns, back to the
beginning.
—Plato

As bad as anyone feared

Max stirred. He was, he slowly realized, on a couch at his own place in Vinegar Hill. A half-empty beer bottle in his lap had dripped most of its contents onto his pants. The coffee table in front of him was so full of empties he was hard-put to place this one on it. Also his hand was shaking so the movement tumbled other bottles. Two hit the floor and rolled. The others clanged on each other—a sound that rocketed around his head like knives on a Roman chariot wheel. There was also a loud ringing sound.

"Is anyone here?" he croaked.

No reply.

"Hello!" he tried again.

He turned his throbbing head toward the table. Chairs were tossed over. Beyond it the kitchen sink looked full of dirty dishes, ashtrays, food containers, more empties. The room bobbed and circled. He realized it was daytime.

"What day?"

No reply. How many days had it been?

"What the fuck?"

A phone was ringing. It had been ringing. Ringing had made him open his eyes and this continued ringing made him shut them again.

"Christ! I need a drink," he announced to no one, picking up a crumpled *Daily News* on the floor at the end of the couch.

"February 3?" The small print at the top was spinning. His eyes or his head? Was this paper old or new? What day is it now?

The phone stopped.

I better pee, he realized, before I pee myself, and managed to strip his wet pants, but he fell down on his way to the john and had to crawl to the bathroom doorway before he could pull himself up. The bathroom looked like a rock concert audience had been there before him. Bottles and cans were everywhere and someone had thrown up in the sink. He managed not to gag. Before his long pee ended, the phone started ringing again.

Max found the phone under a fat pile of fliers, each with Britz's large pale eyes looking directly out at him. The caller was Theo.

"Max!" He was clearly crying. "The cops are trying to reach you. They've found, they've found something. They need you. I'll be there as soon as I can. Wait for me. Please. I can't go with them by myself."

Adrenaline battled with alcohol while Max showered and dressed. He found his dark glasses and amazingly his wallet and keys. He was waiting by the door when the phone rang again.

"It's Eddy," the caller said. "Eddy from across the street."

"What the fuck do you want?"

"Listen, guy, keep your hair on. I want to tell you Burton has a signed broadside from the Captive Lion Press.

It's signed and it's dated and it backs Burt's claim. I just want you to be aware that he's taken it to his lawyers. Theo, Britz, and you'll be hearing soon."

"Signed?"

"Yes. Clear as day: J. Nexfield."

"Signed? I don't get what you're saying."

"Are you deaf? Are you drunk?"

"Why are you calling me?"

"You *are* drunk. Your buddy Theo Henneberg and his fuckin' prize-winning novel! You guys are gonna get it big-time."

"Why are you...what. Don't you know Britz is MISSING!" Max stumbled to the icebox, inadvertently pulling the telephone cord out of the wall plug. The phone went dead but the beer he retrieved rolled down his throat cold and heaven-sent until it crashed into the flood of adrenaline in his gut. He was still trying to replug the phone when a cop car stopped by the front gate and Theo scrambled out.

§

A body had been found on the shore of Fort Hancock, Sandy Hook, New Jersey. The far away mouth of the harbor. A female body, wearing clothing that matched the description Max and Lois had provided. It had been in the water three weeks. They were now headed to Family Counseling, the cops called it. For visual identification. The Staten Island morgue.

"You'll be able to recognize if this is your missing family member," said the cop in front passenger seat. "The water's been pretty cold."

"We need your I.D. to get an investigation started," the driver explained.

"I told you," Theo cried out to them. "I can't, I can't."

"I'm not in good shape," Max added which was obvious. "What, this body was just washed up? Someone found it? Who? "

"You'll get the report from the counselor."

"We're going where?"

"Seaview Hospital. The Jersey cops motored the remains over from the Hook."

"No," Theo said. "No, no."

"Cut it out Theo," Max ordered. "We don't know anything yet."

The cop car was making time down the BQE, heading for the Verrazano Bridge. Max tried not to watch the roadway heaving in the bright sun or the glittering harbor showing itself periodically to his right. He held his head down, away from the blasts of light.

"Just breathe, Theo." They held hands finally, as the car soared over the high gray-blue arch spanning the Narrows. They kept holding hands as the cop car threaded through domestic streets, commercial corners, then scattered parcels of empty woods and fallow farm fields until the cop pulled into a hospital parking lot.

§

It was Britz. On the morgue's steel table. Her face looked as if it had been dipped in paraffin, preserved like something for Madame Tussaud's. It was bloated and pale and she was very dead. She did not look like she was sleeping.

The rest of her body was covered with a white modesty cover. Even so Max could tell her clothing had been removed. Two bare feet of mottled blue poked out at the end of the sheet, and a paper I.D. label was wired to one of the big toes.

"It's a post-mortem wax," the counselor said gently. "It's nothing we did. It happens when the water's very cold."

"What happened." It was more statement than question. Max wasn't exactly sober but he was icy cold as he took a seat in the overheated interview room. The window to the viewing area had been closed. Theo, shivering uncontrollably, had been given a silver rescue blanket.

"We need Mr. Henneberg's signature and we take the remains to the City Medical Examiner for a full report," their counselor said. She was a middle-aged Hispanic woman, with short black-dyed hair and a gold crucifix at her plump neck.

"Are there any marks on her?" Max asked. When they stood next to the morgue table he'd reached over, pulled the white cover down to see but it was only a blur before he'd been stopped by a burly attendant.

"How long will this take?"

"We do best we can, Mr. Billwissil. We understand. We're sorry for your loss, sir."

"Birtwhistle."

"Sorry, Mr. Burlwasel," she tried again.

"Can't we take her home?" Theo wailed. "She's my sister."

"She's not alive, Theo. She's not here," said Max. "Can you get us back to Vinegar Hill. Please."

What to tell, what to hide

"Theo, I know where Britz was when you two were out of touch."

Theo gaped. They had collapsed together in Max's filthy place, barely taking off their respective winter coats.

"She told me," Max persisted. "I'm not sure how much of this to tell anyone else." He was seeing a vivid image of her as he'd seen her for the very first time. It was a noisy after-theater party in a Canal Street loft. Full of theater people, dancers, hangers-on, a few artists, lots of drugs. The party had followed an hypnotic multimedia concert at The Kitchen. Everyone was stunned, electrified, stoned, even those who never used a thing. Max had loved it, but he couldn't quite remember who he had come with when he saw thin, pale, utterly self-possessed Britz, threading through the mob carrying three tall paper cups of something with ice and vodka. She was bringing the drinks to him. She was as cool as the drinks, and interested in him, he knew immediately. Yes, he had gone there with Theo. She was bringing a drink for each of them. Was it Theo who had wanted them to meet?

"This is my big sister," Theo had said, beaming.

Britz. The image swam. He could see her face post-orgasm, and then pre-breakfast. He saw her deeply concentrated face reading at his kitchen table, and then with her head thrown back and eyes wrinkled shut in a full body laugh.

"Did she never tell you?" Max asked.

"She *can't* be dead," said Theo.

Max pulled Theo into a full hug, almost lifting his slight body onto Max's lap. Theo pulled his fingers through Max's tangled hair and held for a beat but then determinedly pushed himself off and up using a hand on Max's shoulder knob. He headed for the kitchen counter.

"I need to do something. Please. Just come over here," he insisted. Hot water. A sponge. Theo began separating garbage from dishes and Max parked himself on a stool just opposite.

Max began. "She told me she ran away from her parents when she was eighteen. Very strict Christians, I guess. Evangelicals? Everything was a sin."

"Yes. Mostly true."

"She had run away but she hadn't left the town. No money. She had a plan to work in a local restaurant. They were going to let her live in a room upstairs. Your parents caught up with her the very next day, your parents did, and had her arrested."

Theo jumped.

"Just hold on." Max pushed a pile of dirty coffee cups toward the sink. "It got very ugly. They told the authorities Britz had lost her mind. For all I know, they really believed it. She was telling them she didn't believe in God, that Jesus was just a man not a god, and she told me she told the cops that she didn't want to live with her parents any more. It all happened pretty fast after that. The cops and your parents took her to a courthouse somewhere nearby, got a local sawbones, and whatever was required back then, and she was involuntarily committed to the state lunatic asylum. It was Tennessee, you know. Deep rural Tennessee. Where you'd have to be crazy if you said you didn't believe in God. And she wasn't twenty-one, not even close, so legally she was totally under her parents."

"And she said she didn't believe in God," Theo whispered. "No wonder they left me locked in the house." After a pause, his eyes already red from tears began to water again.

"So that's where she was. The asylum was a pretty big place, she told me, couple of hundred inmates, way out in the country somewhere," Max went on, "Not that that would have mattered. People from your Farm commune wouldn't have been able to do a thing about it. They were gonna be run out of the county pretty soon as it was. So Britz, you know her, she told me she just kept her head down. The big threat was electroshock and it happened often enough. She started befriending people, making herself useful. The guards and cooks and cleaners. She said the inmates were mostly pathetic. A lot of them were retarded, others were crazed, and a few completely psycho. The employees were products of the same superstitions and poor nutrition as the inmates is how she put it to me. She saw a lot of cruelty. Point is how could she ever get out? She'd have to be twenty-one to even have her own hearing. Three years. And then what? No guarantee they'd believe her no matter what story she told."

"How long was she in there?" Theo rumbled almost inaudibly.

"She lost track of time she told me. I'm sure she was seriously depressed. She knew that winter was coming on. So one afternoon she stole a winter coat from one of the cooks. She put it on and just walked out. I guess the guards knew her so well by then they almost forgot she was an inmate. She told me she said 'goodnight, Woody' to the guy at the gate and walked down the driveway. It took a lot of self-control not to run. She got out to the highway and walked there too. She walked until it was quite dark and she was so cold that she took the risk of hitching and stuck out her thumb for a ride."

"Holeee shit," said Theo.

"Here's the part that's crazy magic, even for Britz. This young man picks her up. Says he's a college student going back to school in Michigan. Been visiting his grandparents. I think it was just past Thanksgiving. He sees she's shivering so he drives into a Howard Johnson for hot coffee and some food. While she's eating she blurts out her story. Under the coat all she's got on is a kind of pinafore. No buttons. Just ties in the back. And that's it. Inmates didn't get underwear. No shoes just rubber slippers. Then he says he has to make a phone call and leaves her sitting here. She was that close to making a run for it, but she was so cold and tired she just sat.

"My mother says I'm to bring you home," is what he tells her when he gets back to their booth. And that's what he does. He takes her all the way to Michigan to his parents' home and they take her in. They get her a legal aid lawyer to sort out the commitment stuff. They get her some clothes. She has to stay inside the house until the lawyer says it's okay. After that they help her start school at the community college their son goes to. His mother tells Britz there are not very many chances a person gets in a lifetime to really help someone else, and this was theirs. So she and her husband, they took it. Just like that."

The glasses were sparkling. The dishwasher sloshed quietly. The counter had been mopped and dried.

"What happened, Max? How could something like this happen? How? Why?!"

No answer. Max knew he had to keep calm. Theo made his way back into the big room, and curled himself into a silent fetal ball on the biggest couch.

The world is made of pictures of the world,
And the pictures change the world into another world
We cannot know, as we knew not this one.
—Howard Nemerov,
"Witnessing the Launch of the Shuttle Atlantis"

EVERYBODY'S QUESTIONS

Conner Brady was only half awake. He'd been in a marathon poker game the whole weekend and then pulled a long shift. This is all he needs now. A new missing person report. I.D. looks confirmed. Foul play looks likely. That's about it. It won't go anywhere. Another. Another. Oh yes, he gets told, next of kin is a queer. True to type he's a total hysteric. Plus he's got a sidekick, an older guy. Seems he's the dead woman's current lover or so they say. He might be just as queer. Still he seems a bit more reasonable to deal with than the brother but there's always a chance he's the one who tossed the lady in the drink.

Everything's still waiting for the complete tox report and more about the body. Cause of death still in question. In the harbor three weeks. Lots of injuries but they look postmortem. Was she beaten first or knocked about in the harbor, or both? Could it be a suicide? Did she drown or was she dead when she went in?

I suppose it's good news we got a positive I.D. right away, Conner mused.

He was still brooding over a recent department report on Brooklyn's 1985 murder rates. As of a year ago, it's way higher than back in the 1960s. We're in a spike for whatever reason. Drugs maybe, he's thinking. Worse is the dismal percentage of murder cases solved. After one year, way more than half the total go cold case, meaning nothing nowhere never. Another, another. The solve rates for waterfront Brooklyn's suspicious deaths are among the worst in the borough. Who says you can't get away with murder!

I gotta get out of this racket, Conner thinks, digging for the small tin of Tums in his pants pocket. He's let himself in for a real stomach churn; he's begun counting the units he has to complete before his pension is fully vested.

What kind of shit way is that to think about your life, he sneered at himself. It's been four years since the divorce. Can't seem to connect with the boys any more. They both act bored to death whenever I get together with them. Twelve and fourteen. Guess I remember. Shit I need a beer.

§

Max opened the big door to admit a police detective and a deputy. The detective, a big Irishman, a bit haggard and hunched, was in street clothes; the deputy, a pleasant looking young Chinese woman, was in uniform. Her name tag, Max noticed, said "Nien-jen, S."

"I'm Brady Conner, in charge of investigating the death of Ms. Henneberg. I know this is a very difficult time for you but your input is—" and Max tuned out as the detective went through a routine script. Blah, blah, blah cookie-cutter protocols. The speech even included a semi-Miranda, "anything you say may be taken as evidence" but he didn't suggest Max needs a lawyer.

"Not yet," Max thought bitterly, stifling the cry of "Britz, Britz, Britz!" echoing through his head.

"My partner, Police Officer Nien-jen has a list of questions..."

"Summer," the deputy put in. "Just call me Summer. My parents do." She had a soft Queens accent and an almost smile; she sat down and extracted a notebook and pen from one of her several cargo pockets.

"Is anyone else here?" Conner looked around the space and took a few steps toward the hallway that led to the back bedrooms.

Conner followed closely as Max opened a door to the bedroom where Theo had been sleeping. Then he opened the door to the other one. "No one here. Her brother, Theo? He's probably at..." he began. The phone began violent ringing.

It was Emily Transholm, the V.P. for public affairs at Dawson. She introduced herself to Max and gently offered condolences before launching into the real reason for her call. While he was of course free to cooperate with the police investigation, she was offering—in a don't-turn-this-down fashion—that her department would take over all the interviews the police will require from Dawson-connected people. And Britz Henneberg's brother Theo as well. To ensure privacy. Discretion. She had quickly connected the Henneberg name to the small swell of literary publicity surrounding Theo's just published novel. Of course her people, she promised, would serve as liaison with pertinent staff people at Wellington-Weeks. And provide him, Max, with any support he required vis a vis his gallery or other concerns.

"A tragedy like this is so easily fodder for the media," she sympathized.

Max was jolted more than he expected by her very careful pronunciation of the word 'tragedy.'

"What do you know about it?"

"Oh Max...I am sorry. May I call you Max? The police treat all suspicious deaths like homicides until they can definitely rule it out. It will be *very* trying."

Max said nothing.

"That's why I know you need all the assistance we can give you. We're a big institution and we've had our share of problems, as you may know."

She paused perhaps to see if he recollected a recent scandal involving several months of secret cancer treatment for an important U.S. diplomat who wanted to conceal his ill health. It was all over when he died but even so the Dawson Center's official reports had reported that his death was sudden and totally unexpected.

She dropped his name with a question inflection and no details. Max couldn't have given the dog's breakfast for this. He knew she was trying to enlist him, to prep him for her pitch; he simply waited for her to get into it.

"Theodore's publisher, the Wellington-Weeks people, they will be just as concerned as we are that the news media treat this matter respectfully." She brimmed collegial sympathy.

"Homicide," Max said as if to himself.

"I'd like to send a car over to bring you to my house," she continued. "Would that be okay?"

"The cops are here now, " he said. She drew in a breath.

"You know my position here at Dawson is as much about distraction as, well, it can be just as important to keep things out of the media as it is to get attention from it. The institute's splendid on-going work generally speaks for itself."

"Are you saying I shouldn't talk to them?" Max butted in.

"Nothing of the kind," she almost purred. "You've just had a terrible blow. You need some time and especially some privacy."

"They say they need information, right now."

The two cops, Conner and Summer, were both standing on the other side of his kitchen table, clearly taking note of every word they could hear.

"But of course you're completely free to do whatever seems best for you." She was soft and subtly inviting. Max's shit-detectors were buzzing full blast.

He finally answered: "Look, I'm not sure I'm getting the full story."

"I'm sure you're not," she agreed. "They don't want to discuss what they haven't nailed down. Max, that's what I'd like to talk about with you—in private."

"I think you better call me back. Better still, I'll call you." Max pushed the receiver lever that broke the connection. Then he put the ringer on mute and nodded to Conner and Summer.

"Do I need a lawyer?"

"Why would you need a lawyer?" Conner asked.

"What happened to Britz?"

"Gondelieve?" Summer asked, turning her notebook back a page.

"Why would you need a lawyer?" Conner asked again.

"Everyone calls her Britz. The Gondelieve thing is a special name only her parents use."

"Let's start at the beginning," Conner took charge. "When did you see her last?"

§

For the next twenty or thirty minutes Max gave the two detectives times, dates, names and addresses of friends, neighbors, colleagues, collectors, doctors, all the verifiable data he could think of. He spoke as dryly as he could, and said nothing about Burton's accusations, nothing about the abrasive phone call from Karl Ziek, nothing about the assignment Britz had been working on. He did say how helpful Lois had been Friday night, and that Theo had arrived not too long after Lois had gone home. He did say he thought phone records would back up most of the details of his story. He added that he had the impression Britz had talked to another lab staffer, Shahid Patel, earlier that Thursday evening. He hadn't been in the room at the time but he assumed it was about work they did together at the Dawson Center.

When their questioning was complete Max slammed his hands down on the table and glared.

"Okay, folks. Now you give me: What happened to Britz? I need to know."

Conner plucked another Tums from the tin in his front pocket and Summer picked up Max's phone and dialed a number. She was checking for the latest results from the autopsy room. The call was transferred several times. She

69

answered in monosyllables and waited. Max tried to un-clench his jaw and breathe evenly.

"Mr. Birtwhistle, your girl friend died of a broken neck. The medical examiner said death was instantaneous. She entered the water after death. Definitely not suicide. The M.E. puts the time about the start of her absence here, late Thursday night or very early Friday morning. We'll need statements about your whereabouts and from your friend Lois, and Miss Henneberg's brother, plus corroboration via phone records if that's possible."

"While you're at it, get a statement from the man across the street. Burton MacIllerny. I went there to see if they'd seen her. And I called my friend Gray. Do you need my permission for phone records?"

"Can we call someone for you? This is not a good time to be alone," Conner asked. He was doing his best good-cop, Max thought.

"So what do you have to go on?" Max asked him.

"Not much right now, man. The harbor washed every-thing pretty clean. But we'll learn a lot more from our in-terviews."

"Get on with it then," Max answered. He wanted them out of his house before he called Theo.

"Mr. Birtwhistle," Summer injected. "I know people want to know this even if they don't ask. The autopsy shows she was not raped."

"Please leave now," Max managed with a modicum of cool. He led them to the door and locked it behind them.

Giovanni's Room is not really about homosexuality. It's about what happens to you if you're afraid to love anybody.
—James Baldwin, in a 1980 radio interview

THEO TRIES TO THINK

Theo is in his bedroom on Avenue C. His life continues to be punctuated by the periodic arrival and departure of work crews. Two guys are there now, doing something in the kitchen so they can install a large chef's stove.

"Would you *please* focus on making the bathroom fully functional," Theo begs.

I'm tracking plasterboard dust everywhere, he's thinking. I'm finding broken screws inside my fucking bedroom slippers. Friends keep crashing in. Most know and some don't know about Britz being missing. And now she's dead. Do I have to *tell* them? They all know about my recent—well, my novel and the stir it's making. This apartment is a highway, a construction site, an open sore. I wonder how many of 'em will really *read* my book!

The big electric typewriter on an old walnut table right under a bedroom window is meant to be an oasis for concentration in the midst of uproar. It could be. It can be. It's nothing yet. Maybe he shouldn't ever write anything again.

Friends! I hope none of them are helping themselves. Theo considers his visitors. Who's been here? Mike. Gender Gen. Bruno? Cee, for sure. There's too much loose stuff here. Oh Britz, I haven't got time for this. I do want to write. I just need time to work. Did I tell you about my new book? Did I tell you what's happened? And now I've lost you. Again. I've always lost you. Always. Who else will I ever love?

Theo's tears are rolling again.

"Hey man! Ya hungry?"

It's Clipper, he sees through the water in his eyes, standing at the bedroom door. Clipper who's been crashing here for days. His old man threw him out, Theo remembered. Clipper, who never clips anything. Not hair or toenails but he certainly clips money or food. Theo had forgotten all about him.

"Clipper for chrissake, I told you to get the fuck out! Yesterday. Right?"

"I need some money, man. I'm flat, I'm totally. . ."

"Will you get it! My sister is dead. My house is never finished. My publisher thinks I'm New York's new boy toy. I have a *book* to write. And now I hear my *mother* is coming to New York to get the body. Her. Britz. She's a body now. She's a *body*! Ya gotta leave me alone." It was unusual for Theo to blow off this way, but he is screaming full voice, and Clipper looks stupefied.

I have to stop crying all the time, Theo thinks. I have to think.

"Did Max just tell me the cops are on the way here?" he asks.

"How would I know?" Clipper is rightfully mystified, and hurt. "Jesus, Mary, and Joseph," Clipper looks close to tears. "Theo! Will ya give me some money so I can get somethin!"

"You can go NOW!" Theo is steering his sour-smelling

friend by the elbow, shoving him out of the apartment door and onto the hall landing just as a man in a chauffer's uniform puffs up the last flight of steps, holding his placard, Tru Time Limo. The name Henneberg is scrawled in magic marker on the white space at the bottom.

There a jam as Theo is tries to push Clipper past the limo driver, a hefty man who is not yet on the top step and is clinging tightly to the bannister. Clipper's grip on Theo gives way, he gives up, and screeching "Motherfucker" bumps limply down eight steps to the corner landing. There he regains his feet and with a river of curses, manages the next set of eight steps and disappears. The stairs to the lower floors are in the front. His curses echo upward from the hallway below. The limo driver doesn't flinch.

"Ya fuckin broke my hip, ya lousy bastard. Fuck you. Fuck you." Clipper's voice fades down the hallway of the floor below.

"You Henneberg?" the driver says. "You're wanted at Ms. Transholm's apartment."

Theo covers his eyes with his hand. "I haven't a clue what you're talking about."

Two workmen are standing in his apartment's doorway. One of them has a full set of keys.

"I have to look after this place before I do anything else," Theo tells the driver. "You better tell that Transwhat person I'm not going anywhere."

WHO IS IN CHARGE?

Move them around like chess pieces. That'll make them tell me what they know! This patent leather bitch with her lah-dee-dah apartment wants to control the *police* investigation? Good luck to her.

Max had allowed himself to be transported by limo to Emily Transholm's Upper East Side apartment, taken inside, seated in an exquisitely upholstered easy chair, and supplied with a perfect espresso in a tiny red cup. Max left it on the glass coffee table, along with the proffered tray of biscotti. Emily waltzed about a bit, adjusting the living room curtains, checking the thermostat, shaking out her long blue skirt.

"So exactly what do the police know that they haven't told me?" Max demanded after a long pause.

"Every one of Ms. Henneberg's colleagues is going to be questioned," Emily said softly, "as will the laboratory chief."

"So?"

"I think we might get some snow tonight," she murmured.

"Oh for crying out loud," he burst out. "Of course everyone will be questioned. I've been around the block. What makes you think you're needed in this equation?"

"Max, I'm happy to be a liaison between you and Dawson staff members," she paused while Max glared. "There could be sensitive issues around Dawson Center research projects. The staff will be more comfortable talking to me about such matters." She implied but did not say that she was equipped to understand nuances that might not be obvious to outsiders. There was more. She didn't want him to talk with anybody unless she knew about it, and *ahead of time*. To hide how much this infuriated him, Max calmly asked for the use of her phone. It would be wise to check any messages on his answering machine back in Vinegar Hill, he told himself. He had to admit he felt a little exposed with no one at all back in his Vinegar Hill building.

Before she could comply, her little white telephone phone pealed. The phone ringer was a tiny carillon, delivering a folk song fragment. Max would have laughed if he hadn't been so angry.

"I'm sorry, I have to take this," she said after listening several seconds to what was being said on the other end. Her lips tightened anxiously. The phone cord wasn't long enough to let her retreat to another room and close the door; she had to put the receiver down and cross to a bedroom behind them where there was, evidently, another extension. Max got to his feet beside the chair he'd occupied and stood listening to the white mouthpiece on the small phone table emitting the faraway voice of what he was sure was Dr. Miller, Britz's boss. He was telling someone to spare him any interruption. Max raised his eyebrows at Emily but she avoided eye contact as she swept back into the living room to hang up the phone.

"I do have to take this. Please give me a minute," she

murmured, retreating again. The door closed with a click. It was followed by silence and then by the sound of her very muffled pleading. There was no way to convert the sounds into intelligible words and Max chose not to lift the receiver. Without special equipment, there would be an audible click. There might even be an echo.

The call ended. Emily did not immediately return, and when she did her interest in Max had lost its urgency. He was very aware she now wanted him to leave. For why? Oh, for more phone calls of course or to go somewhere and to whom and for what? That's what I won't get from her, he knew. Just by my being here, she's let me in on more than she wanted. I won't get more. He asked again to use her phone, and accessed his answering machine.

The message from a very hyper Theo reported that he and Max were wanted by Emily Thorn-something, the V.P. of public persuasion at the Dawson. "Take care. Don't go! She's a real witch," Theo insisted. "But we gotta talk! My *mother* is on the way to New York. The bus'll take a few days from New Harmony, maybe two, but..." He broke off to groan. Cops were at his door. "Please meet me here, Max. On Avenue C!"

Instead of that, Max headed over to the Dawson institute. It wasn't his shit detectors, the shivering sensation he often got when someone was lying or bullshitting him, it certainly wasn't fear, the dry mouth, the tight stomach, and it wasn't coherent enough to be called suspicion. It was, he recognized, a crazy possessiveness. Max suddenly wanted all of Britz's personal possessions, the things in her office, the stuff from her desk. Everything that Dawson had that had her smell, that she'd touched, her personal books, her extra sweater. He didn't want them handled by anyone else. He wanted to take everything home.

It wasn't a long walk, but the early afternoon was already dark and it was growing colder by the minute. Snow in the air, or freezing rain. A sanitation truck heaped with salt lumbered by.

Max asked for security as soon as he entered the lab building. Eventually he was escorted to a small office on an underground floor—and dealt with by a sweet-faced old Hungarian—he guessed the nationality by the name tag: "Gyuri Farkis." The old man remembered Britz and his condolences were genuine. What happened? What happened? He shook his head in disbelief.

"I know the cops need to interview everyone who knew her, but I don't think they need her personal stuff. Do they? Her mother's going to be here in a day or two and I'd like to have her personal things home. Look," Max went on, "I can sign for everything I take. You know we were engaged," he lied. "Her mother knows we were planning..."

That was enough. The guard's milky gray eyes filled. He rummaged in a desk drawer and produced a round black bottle labeled Zwack which he used to half-fill two plastic glasses from the water cooler in the corner. "It's a painkiller, my friend," he said and tossed the liquid off in one gulp. Max sniffed his glass and realized he could not possibly sip the stuff, so he followed suit with a rapid gulp.

Before Max could stop him, his cup was refilled.

"It'll stop burning in a minute," said the guard. "When we've had two, we'll go up to her floor. Lovely girl, your girl, always a smile for me," he said.

"God yes," Max replied, finding the second jolt almost comforting. All of middle Europe was conspiring to help him. He could feel waves of warm concern from his German O-Ma, his mother's mother.

"Seventeen herbs," said old Farkis. "Very important."

Back in Detroit, during the war, O-Ma had been his anchor and support while both his parents sucked up all the overtime war-work factories were offering. Sometimes eighteen-hour days for his dad, a bit less for his ma. Even so she'd leave the house before light and not return until after dark, day after day. His dad had lost the little mountain farm his family had worked for so long. Gone to the bank, he had growled at his son, gone after seven generations. "Bank" left a puzzling image in Max's head for years. He'd think of the bank of the crick that bordered the main meadow behind the half-remembered cabin, or the bank of a highway because his dad would say "good banking" while downshifting around a curving mountain road. He'd been a little over four when they left Tennessee, and his memories were distorted by adult stories, by his dad's tightlipped grief, by his mother's determined stoicism. The money too. Another bank; it was all banked. During the war everything they made they saved, though no one ever said they might someday go back to the farm. It was gone. It was past. It had died.

The burn of the Zwack then spiked a replay of the daily hostility of kids in his grandmother's Detroit neighborhood. She was a *German*, a fact betrayed every day out on the street by her heavily accented English. Safe at home, her German was mellifluous, and she often sang in it. It sounded nothing like the guttural achtung sounds of Nazis with guns and dogs featured in the films at the Lowes kids' matinee on Saturdays.

He accepted a third refill and slowly floated.

§

"You can't bring that man in here!" Karl Ziek barreled into what had been Britz's cubbyhole of an office and shouted at the old security guard. "Nothing is to be taken. Who told you!"

Farkis straightened the lanyard holding his I.D., pulled out his pager, and called the security chief, completely unimpressed by Karl's outburst.

"Just personal things. Her mother will be here tomorrow," he said calmly into the walkie-talkie. "I'll take a list." He began folding open the flat cardboard containers he'd brought with him. Karl grabbed at the containers and moved as if to push the security guard back toward the lab door. Max stared, sobered a bit by this display.

"What's the matter with you Karl?" Winston demanded. "For godsake man, Britz *died*." Almost immediately Ji-yoo was standing right behind him, looking just as horrified.

"There's an inquiry going on. You the one who's crazy," Karl snarled at Winston.

"Not for you to decide," Ji-yoo injected. She was not a person one wants to insult out of hand. She, after all, was the lab manager. "You should have called me first!" she said to Farkis.

"He's Miss Henneberg's fiance. Just arrived. It's close to five. Any inconvenience I apologize," he told her. "Only personal items. Mr. Kingston will have my list."

79

"You're not taking anything!" Karl roared. "This guy has papers Henneberg took from the lab weeks ago and he refuses to give them back!"

"What's the big concern over those papers, Ziek?" Max demanded of Karl. "I've given them to the investigating detectives" he lied.

"No you didn't," Karl sputtered.

"So Max, my friend, do you see the things you want?" Old Farkis was beyond cool. Karl could have been a badly behaved dog, if that. He was certainly not Farkis's problem.

"Give him the cartons, now" Ji-yoo snapped at Karl.

"Thank you," Max smiled at her. "I just want, well, those photographs. I think she had a few books. And a little ceramic jar I gave her. Her sweater. We don't even know what arrangements her mother will want. Or when we can do.... But I'll call you," he trailed off.

"We are so...we feel terrible," Ji-yoo said and unexpectedly and seemingly out of character she reached up and kissed Max on the cheek. "You apologize," she demanded of Karl. He did not.

"We'll see," he said finally, as Max and Farkis were leaving. He folded his heavy arms across his wide chest and glared, "We'll see."

It had begun to snow in earnest as Max trudged to the subway carrying just one box. Britz had been her usual abstemious self, protecting her personal life and stocking her bench and cubby with very few personal things. Life-long habits, Max thought sadly. Never at home, never unguarded, always ready to move again. The pain of her life thumped at his chest. *Who took her from me? I don't* just need to know. I want the person who did this to pay. I want the payment to be something incredibly important to him, or they, or whatever!

> . . . get on with it, keep moving, keep in speed, the
> nerves, their speed, the perceptions, theirs, the acts,
> the split second acts, the whole business, keep it mov-
> ing as fast as you can, citizen.
> —Charles Olson, from *Projective Verse*

CONNER OUT OF THE CORNER

It was dark. It was snowing. Another bleak weekend was about to begin. I'm no detective, Max was thinking. The last time I got involved in pursuing answers to a murder it ended in more killing, needless deaths too, and it ended with no one winning, it ended with me vowing to never do it again. Ach, but then I waded in because of a friend. His trouble. This is different. I don't have to wade in. I'm drowning in it anyway. He kicked his door open. Then slammed it. He kicked a chair that was in his way. He stopped himself from banging into one of the big support pillars that held up the roof and fumbled for the private number Conner Brady had given him.

Max sat in his studio, drawing a kind of diagram, as he held the ringing phone. How is a homicide investigated? he drew in heavy black block letters. Then he turned his pen to the side for a lighter graphic:

1. The victim. Lifestyle, habits, relationships, employment, personality, leisure activities, drug use, alcohol use, sex life.
2. The crime scene.
3. Forensic evidence. From the body (toxicology, hair, DNA) and from the crime scene (fingerprints, powder

burns, spent shells, blood spatter, signs of struggle, ef-
forts to alter).
4. Witnesses.

He crossed out numbers 2 and 4 because no crime
scene, no witnesses. He crossed out most of the list of
crime-scene forensics for the same reason. Didn't exist.
Not known.

Conner's phone kept ringing. Shit, it is Friday night.
The guy could have a life, Max thought. He was about to
disconnect when a drowsy voice said "Yoh."

"Got some time?" he asked. "It's Max Birtwhistle. Listen, Brady, do you find gossip useful in a case like this one
or are you strictly seeking hard evidence?"

"There's no fucking hard evidence, man. Except what
the M.E. said. She didn't do this to herself."

Max could hear muffled sounds, throat clearing, then
the scratching of a match. Brady was waking up to a cigarette.

"Is this a bad time? Am I intruding?"

"No, no, no man. I was uh takin' a nap. Whatta you
wanna tell me?"

"I'd rather meet face to face. Are you in Brooklyn?"

"As a matter of fact, I'm cooping upstairs at the Gold
Street precinct."

Max felt a pang as he remembered the place—the station house where he'd first reported Britz as missing. He
also remembered a bar near Boro Hall where newsmen
liked to hang out if a juicy trial was in progress or some
Brooklyn scandal was breaking. He described the place
and asked if Brady would meet him there in about an hour.

"It's still snowing, but it should be close enough to

Gold to walk it," he ended. If Brady knew the place he didn't twig, just grunted acknowledgments of Max's directions.

For Max the walk was somewhat longer. The sting of cold helped center him again. The city quiets down wonderfully with a small layer of fresh snow. Where do the cars disappear to? By the time he reached the bar it was already letting up a bit leaving sparkling frosting on building fronts and a slightly crunchy two-three inches on the sidewalk. The bar was there as remembered, with dirty windows and lots of wood paneling inside, lit by yellowed light globes hanging from the ceiling. It was now very cold. Brady Conner was already there. A whisky drinker, Max noted with pleasure. Even though the place was hardly crowded, they moved from the bar to a booth.

"Has anything like this happened in this area recently?" Max asked.

"Like what?"

"Attacks? Maybe bag snatching gone wrong? No one's found her bag. She left our place around ten. Then she was in the water for days and days. What happened in the time between? From when she left our place and when the ME thinks.... Could she have taken the subway? Have the token booth people been questioned, shown her photo?

"Done. No hits," Conner answered.

"Could she have gone somewhere in a car? It doesn't make any sense."

"The river's easy to reach down Dock Street," Conner said softly, "We have pretty good data on what the harbor currents do, so she wouldn't necessarily have to be taken away from Dumbo to end up out there on Sandy Hook."

He looked at Max's hands after a pause, "But yeah, it could also have been a kidnapping. Do you know anything to support that? Enemies?"

"There are things I haven't told you," Max began.

"Yep," Brady said. "By the way, it's Conner. You're Max to me."

"I don't know if this has anything to do with what happened to Britz, but something is buggy at the Dawson Center. I went there to get her personal things and one of the lab techs just lost it. He was already in snit right after she went missing. Wanting come out to our place for some work papers she'd taken home. God, I still thought she was alive, she'd turn up. Not strange I guess. I mean I heard from Britz those lab scientists can get whack-oh about secrecy, credit for their findings. Still this gave me a turn. Ever dealt with scientists?"

"A little," came the laconic reply.

"I lied and told him I'd given the papers to you. And man that really rattled him. And there's another thing. The neighbors right across the street, Burton and Eddy, they have a beef with Britz's brother. Theo has published a novel that has a whole passel of literary folks excited. Burton is a writer too, they know a lot of the same people. He and Eddy made a big scene at our place about a week before Britz went missing, accusing Theo of plagiarism. Britz is, oh god, she *was*, Theo's protector. It got so bad I had to throw them out of the house. Personally I don't think there's anything to it but jealousy. You do get it they're all gay?"

He knew he was taking a chance passing this on but figured Conner would pick it up anyway as soon as he saw

Burton and Eddy. I just have to hope Conner has some reasonable acceptance of human behavior. You never know though, he thought.

He went up to the bar to buy two more drinks, telling himself I'll find out for sure when I bring the drinks back. So I took a chance, he consoled himself. Truth is I don't care. I don't care if it scorches Theo I mean. I have to find the bastard. Maybe it's bastards. I have to find who did this. Suppose Burton and Eddy were involved?

Max knocked back one of the two drinks, ordered a replacement, and then realized he needed to eat.

"Hey Conner, want something?" he called over to their booth. "I'm getting a burger."

§

By the time the bartender announced a one a.m. quitting time to the four remaining customers, the kitchen had closed and Conner and Max had consumed a great deal of bar whiskey, moderate amounts of bar food, and exchanged a lot of personal data. Conner had spent his boyhood nearby, in Red Hook in the old old days. Until his dad, like so many of the Irish immigrants in the neighborhood, passed tests, scored recommendations from men he went to mass with, and snagged a good starting post with the police. After a while he'd moved his family to Long Island. "We're all cops or firemen," he laughed. "The cliché is totally true."

"So you're second generation."

"Never gave a thought to doing anything else. Not then. It's different now." He told Max about his dead-end marriage.

"I was working missing persons, it's a bit of a plum, ya know, high road to top detective. Way above my dad. So I was off on cases all times of the day and night and she couldn't stand it. Now she's married to an accountant. He's home every day at six. Home to the fucking suburbs. Don't know why my ex or my parents either, were so god-damn hot for burbs. I hated leaving the Hook. They used to barbeque out on the street in the Hook. Everybody did. We kids had the run of the waterfront. But lawns! Pain in the ass. What for? My wife didn't give a rat's ass for lawns or garden shit. All she ever wanted to do was hang with her girlfriends and do each other's hair. Now my boys are growing up just as empty as she is. I wish to God they were interested in *something*," he mourned. "I started thinking way too late and that's exactly what they're gon-na do. Unless they never do."

Jesus, Max thought. How's this morose broken-heart-ed man gonna get to the bottom of Britz's murder? Is he planning to sink into drink? One more thing to feel sorry for himself about?

"Look, Conner, I'm an artist, a painter. No joke, failure is part of my game. Comes with the territory, believe me. My parents couldn't believe I'd use the money I saved up shipping out for *art* school. It'd a been easier if I hadda tell them I was a queer. Still there was no way I'd stay in Detroit, do the assembly line. But from art you learn if it fucks up, you have to start again. And sometimes that's the best part...when you start again because it's not the same again. Follow?" After a pause Max steeled himself and blurted his big question: "So Conner, what can I do to help? What can I find out for you?"

"Well, Max my friend, we're not altogether sure *you* didn't do her."

"I'm outta here!" Max began shoving his arms into his coat, restraining a bulging unspoken "fuck you!" This was the second time in one day he'd been called 'my friend' which along with the vile accusation gave his self-control a body blow.

"I do have one question," Conner said. "Who is James Nexfield?

Whoosh. Max sat down.

"It's okay," he called over to the barkeep. He realized that the other two men who'd been at the bar had already left. "We better walk," he told Conner and as they left he began to flesh out the whole story of Burton's accusations.

"Did you hear any of this when interviewing him?" Max asked. "I don't know if anyone else believes him. Obviously there's money involved. And reputations. Scandal could be bad or good for selling a book. Theo's already been in the tabloids. But Britz wasn't involved at all."

He and Conner were walking in the general direction of Gold Street. Snow had stopped. The wind was up, and it was bitter. No gloves. Max shoved his hands into the pockets of his coat. His right hand closed around the key to Britz's old apartment. He'd used that key when he searched there, was it two? three weeks ago? The cold metal worked as a kind of talisman, a charm to keep him focused.

"Britz didn't know any more about James Nexfield than I do. She was shocked nearly senseless when Theo told her he'd taken the man's manuscript," Max said.

Once again he recognized he was taking a chance but Christ I need this guy to trust me and I need to trust him, he repeated to himself. I hope to hell he's worth it.

But the moment a bird was dead, no matter how beautiful it had been in life, the pleasure of possession became blunted for me.
—John James Audubon

A voice
from the long ago Midwest

There was a bunch of messages from Theo on Max's phone. Freaking about the imminent arrival of Britz's mother. Would he please, please, please come with him to meet her? Plus two messages from someone called Dennis Strangleford. It was way too late to call him back, but Max did reach out to Theo. Okay. Mrs. Henneberg wasn't due until the next afternoon. They'd meet at Port Authority bus station, Max agreed. No, Theo had never heard of Strangleford.

§

Max did hear. His phone rang at 8:30 the next morning and a low diffident voice with Midwestern cadences introduced himself. "Dennis, Dennis Strangleford. Folks call me Den."

The police had contacted him in Michigan. A missing-persons specialist found a never-completed divorce decree in Manhattan municipal records. Filed by Gondelieve Henneberg Strangleford. That had to be Britz. It was all correct except for payment of the fee. Her check had bounced. Follow-up mailings were returned undelivered.

Somehow the papers had been filed anyway.

"Don't know why we never finished it," said the man on the phone ruefully, "but there it is; I guess I'm still her husband. It's been eight years I think. I'm surprised they found me to tell you the truth. I'm in Muskegon, but I'm on the road a lot. I consult for a bunch of water authorities on this side of the lake. I'm a wastewater chemist."

You're telling me too much, Max thought. "Yeah, yeah," he said into the phone.

"Look, they gave me your name. I guess she was living with you? We never completed our papers. I guess neither of us cared that much, but I do have a responsibility. I guess..."

"Slow down," Max said. "You were married?"

"We married right after we graduated, here in Michigan."

Max needed a good strong cup of coffee, which was not at hand. "You married in Michigan?"

"We sure were kids! We were both twenty-two. But we never lived here. I hadda go to grad school in Boston. Didn't *have* to but the school gave me this scholarship. Truth is I wasn't too easy in my mind about moving all the way east, I can tell you. I guess I wanted her to come with me. So we married. Anyways, after a while Britz got herself into M.I.T. God she was smart."

"Well, how long..." Max asked.

"We had a hard time, I guess. I hated Boston. I hated everything being so dirty. It was so hard to drive. Parking was worse. We called it quits after oh two years, maybe. I wanted to go home and she, she wanted her molecular biology. Listen, Max, um...."

"Birtwhistle," he supplied

"Sorry about this but if she, well as her husband, if there's a matter of property, don't ya know."

"For god's sake man, we haven't even had a funeral yet. The police are still holding her body. Her mother is due here sometime tomorrow."

"Guess I am being kind of uh. Should I come to New York?"

"What do you want me to say? Suit yourself. Look, she has a bank account. The Dawson Center has employee benefits. Dawson Center. You can look it up. If you want her dough, just get the information yourself. I have no say in this. I'm not married to her." He put the phone down quietly.

Of course she didn't tell me everything. Never mentioned a Den. But why should she? He sounds like a jerk. Even Theo doesn't know about this. She told me the biggest thing in her life was finding Theo after almost ten years, finding him free of their parents and their cults, finding him right here, living in New York City. She was at the Strand bookstore. She was browsing near that big counter in the back where they buy books. There he was selling some art books. Crazy accident.

And now her mother's due. I feel like Theo. I want someone to go with me!

It takes a long time to become young.
—attributed to Pablo Picasso

On the way to Port Authority

Theo had stuffed some clean clothes into a paper shopping bag and was thinking as he walked to Rose Ann's place about a time not so long ago when he'd seen eight in the morning only as an unexpected light breaking in on a long night, never as the beginning of a fresh day.

Not exactly fresh. Last night's snow had already been festooned with soot, dog piss, cigarette butts, and great wings of filthy slush tossed up from the street by passing cars and trucks. Only a few neighborhood sidewalks were shoveled, but the worst obstacles were the dark ponds at every corner. Cold, black, and possibly deep. If jumping over failed, they could desecrate socks, trousers, even suck off a shoe. Theo imagined being taken to an icy nether world. But he had to be early. He knew Beth had gone to Ohio to visit family and Rose Ann had an early morning tutoring gig. So he'd called her. She said she'd leave their extra key with the deli guys across the street from her building. He could have the bathroom in privacy.

"Just clean up a little Theo. Before you leave. I don't want to see any hairs in my soap. Remember this is a favor!"

Lord these lezzies sure are a prissy bunch, Theo snickered to himself. He'd been a bathroom itinerant for weeks and weeks, using a motley array of facilities offered by friends while his apartment renovations were underway but this morning was different. He didn't know what would happen. He'd last seen his mother eleven years ago. Eleven years and what? five lifetimes? The break had been his cross-county hitch from California; he did it to connect with a band because of what the band's music meant to him. That was what Halcyon had done for him. He'd found things for himself while he was there and he'd become convinced that he could make moves on his own. Connection was everything these new mentors told him! He could and he should go and be with the things that moved him.

So he had split to DC to be with the Bad Brains. Theo had found one of their first records and for the first time in his life had been electrified by something other than language in a book. Music! For all that his family had lived in the South much of his life he'd had almost no contact with black people or black music, let alone hear anything like the Brains' ecstatic mix of punk, rock, and Rastafarian. He was consumed; he listened to the side over and over and knew just from sinking into their sounds that they would take him in. It would totally be their ethic. He'd take photographs, he plotted. He'd begun to work with a fine second-hand Leica in Halcyon. He'd find a way to sell his photos for money—to fan publications, record companies, maybe even newspapers.

But by the time he reached Washington, the Brains had left for New York. They'd been banned in D.C. for what the authorities called "out of control" concerts. Theo stayed anyway, as there were other people hanging out in the Brains' former place. He stayed and did begin taking photographs in clubs and out on the street. And checking out various drugs. He found himself in New York only later. By then he found himself wanting to write, not photograph. Words, words always, words all ways. Undone without Britz in his life, he had nevertheless gone on. He hadn't stayed nineteen forever.

What was his mother now? He conjured up her face, adding a decade. I wonder how she'll act if I tell her I left her house to live in a place called Madam's Organ! The house name was a pun on the D.C. neighborhood name, Adams Morgan. He was grinning walking west toward the subway lines as he remembered comings and goings back there. How many changes had his mother gone through since she and his dad had hauled off to Halcyon. What else had they done besides leaving Britz locked up as a lunatic? And where in hell was Dad? Why was he not coming for this unimaginably awful rendezvous?

We've all lost Britz this time, Theo told them in his mind. She ran away from you. She left me. I know now she couldn't come back for me the way she promised because you two had locked her up. You threw her away! But first I lived for years thinking she'd abandoned me. Very bad shit to go through. Now someone else has thrown her away, this time forever. This time I won't find her again. You won't either. So ma, how are you gonna say hello to me after all that? I'm hanging on to what I can keep inside me. That's where Britz is. Right, Britz?

He felt the strange warm pulse in the back of his chest. It had been slowly growing ever since seeing the cold plastic husk of Britz lying on the morgue table.

What or who are you and Dad? his inside voice continued. Do you even deserve to mourn? What are you planning to do? Smile? Cry? Beg forgiveness? Maybe pray? Quote your latest guru? I'm sure there's a new one. There always is.

Theo could feel himself crusting over. His tears were so over. The icy ball of loss in his gut was not receding, rather it had extended down through his feet and out to the ends of his fingertips. It was no longer lodged in his throat. Ice had spread almost evenly behind his eyes, into his brain, ears, belly, genitals. The warm blue pulse he felt was somewhat higher. Radiating behind his solar plexus, insuring that he breathe. Since the visit to the morgue he found he could watch himself and others as calculating as if he were a diamond cutter. It was a very new feeling—this knowing that he could take his time even in the grip of powerful emotions.

Theo soaked in the tub and then shaved and trimmed his hair at Rose Ann and Beth's sink, mopping up everything afterwards. He hung up their towels, scrubbed out the ring on the tub, and remembered to wipe the cake of soap.

Important for old Max to be with me, to meet my mother, not to hold me up or share my terror but because Max needs to know more, Theo was thinking. Max, Theo recognized, needed him.

Inside the mirror resides my doppelganger.
—traditional Punjabi saying

BRITZ TWICE

Max's mouth went dry. The slender woman with silver-gray hair walking toward the glass bus terminal door could have been Britz perhaps twenty years older. My age, Max thought with a pang. It was nearly unbearable. She was wearing a long cotton skirt that fell loosely down almost to feet in well-used hiking boots. For protection against February she had a thick poncho, apparently pieced together from a kaleidoscope of heavy woolen scraps. And a black knit cap. Her poncho was held in place by the straps of her backpack. She was wearing pink mittens and carrying a black satchel with wide wooden handles.

"This is all I have," she called out to Max and Theo, as she came through the door into the terminal ground floor. They were standing somewhat back from the door, allowing dazed passengers to stream by them.

"I don't have to wait out there for a bag."

She marched over to Theo and put her hands on his shoulders.

"Well, son, a terrible occasion to bring us back face to face," she said.

"Yes," he said. She and Theo locked eyes for a brief moment before she let him go and turned to Max.

"You are going to have to find out why she was taken

from us. You're the painter, Max Birtwhistle. I believe my daughter found a harbor in you. A soul place."

Max's mouth was too dry for him to reply, if he'd had one. What had Theo told her about him? He looked into her pale face and light eyes, ringed with brown brows and lashes, then reached down to take the satchel from her.

"Not necessary," she said. "Theo, do we take a subway or a bus? Please lead us out."

It was a long subway ride to Vinegar Hill, and the three of them rode wordlessly. Mrs. Henneberg was completely at ease, hands in her lap, booted feet crossed decorously. Theo sat in almost the same semi-Yoga position. Max moved to an empty seat opposite and watched them both through half-closed eyes.

The replay of Britz shimmered on. It didn't dissipate once they'd entered Max's building, divested themselves of outside clothing, and seated themselves at the kitchen table while Max made tea.

Under the poncho, the cotton dress was softly smocked around the neckline. She scooped up long gray hair freed of the woolen cap, twisted it in loose ball at the nape of her neck and speared it expertly with a large tortoiseshell hairpin.

She broke the silence: "You are going to have to find out why she was taken from us," she repeated, fixing Max with her pale eyes.

"Where is Dad?" Theo interrupted.

"He hasn't been in touch for a while," she said.

"What does that mean?"

"He went on a walk-about in September. I heard from him once. Early November. He was in New Mexico, near the border. He sounded as if he'd go on south. Leave the country."

"Nothing since?"

"Our paths have diverged quite a bit, Theo. This wasn't his first long absence." She turned from Theo and fixed on Max again: "What do you know about my daughter's murder?"

"Not enough. Not even where it happened."

"Tomorrow you'll take me around," she said. "It has been almost five weeks, but this area doesn't seem heavily travelled and there might be something."

"It has been searched and prodded everywhere. By me, by Theo, by several of our friends and by cops, professional search teams. Nothing at all."

"Nothing physical, I understand. I'm considering vibrations. We leave traces of our actions everywhere we go."

"You know, ma, I'm not exactly ready for your mystic malarkey. Where was all this fucking sensibility when you had Britz locked up in the state looney bin? How could you!" Theo stood over his mother, his eyes almost black with demand.

"I wonder about that myself, son. I believe I was under a dark influence."

"*Damn* right it was dark. What were you, drugged?"

The telephone was ringing violently. It was Dr. Judah Miller from Dawson.

"I have company. But I'll call you right back," Max said, suddenly wanting to step away from the mother-son confrontation. It was also much better to have a conversation with Miller in the privacy of his bedroom where he had another extension.

To know the causes of things.
        —Motto of the London School of Economics,
from Virgil, Book 2 of the *Georgics*

HOT PAPER?

Max had expected Miller to offer formal condolences or maybe information about the Center's plans for a memorial for Britz. The voice on the phone was harassed, hoarse, and bare of any sympathy.

He started without preamble: "When Ms. Henneberg was last at the Center she was given documents relating to important clinical trials," Dr. Miller said.

"Yes," Max answered. "I know she had an assignment from you. She told me."

"We need those papers back ASAP. And with any notes she made about them."

"I'm not sure I understand," Max said slowly. "She took copies only, from your central computer, and she told me she signed for everything she brought home."

"I'm not disputing that. I'm saying we need them back ASAP, with her notes."

"Look, Dr. Miller. She didn't finish the job. She... She was still working on it on the Thursday she went missing. The cops say that was the day she died." It was hard to keep his voice level and he decided it would be okay to let the man know that his phone call was making Max angry. He let his voice rise: "I think I need to know what your problem is. You have originals of every item she took. If she made any notes, they might be in her computer, her personal computer, I have no idea. I do know I've no intention of giving her computer to you." As he spoke he was wondering if she'd penciled in any notes on the printouts. He'd look just as soon as he could end this call.

"This is an extremely important matter." Miller was also allowing his voice to rise. "These clinical trials support an FDA application for a possibly life-saving treatment. A treatment benefiting untold thousands. A treatment that will be offered in every accredited emergency facility around the globe! Millions. Millions at stake!"

"Money or people?" Max waited to see if his jab did anything.

"I don't need theatrics from you. I need the papers and the notes, *now*!" Miller yelled.

"No."

There was a moment of silence. "You can expect to be served a court order by tomorrow morning," Dr. Miller announced and banged the phone down.

On what basis, Max wondered. He rang Brady Conner. "I want you to have these papers...today. Can you send for them? Where are you?"

"If you can't bring them over to Gold Street yourself, get a messenger," Conner replied and then, "Hey, are you okay?"

"No. I'm not. The lab head, Miller, threatened a court order. I can't think why he'd be able to get one, except that he's from the Dawson Center and I'm not."

"You got that one right. Get 'em over here. STAT. And, uh, Max, can you open your girl's computer?"

"I don't think so. She might have written her access code down somewhere, but it wouldn't be like her."

"Please bring it too."

Damn, Max realized. He wasn't even sure where Britz had put the papers. A lot had gone on in his place for those three weeks. Maybe twenty people had come in and out. He'd been drunk out of his mind for many of those days. Well, none of the people, thank God, had any connections to Dawson. At least he didn't think so, as a small burn of paranoia suddenly snaked around his belly. He thanked Conner and began a systematic search.

Of course the phone rang. Again. This caller was Emily Transholm, the Dawson's PR person. Again. She purred reassurances of all sorts.

"I haven't got time for this," he interrupted her flow.

"Max, we want to hold a dignified memorial service. The university's faculty club has offered space and catering..."

"I'm not...."

"I daresay you don't understand," she interrupted back. "The FDA application is critical for the continued progress of this amazing new trea..."

"Look, I'm not releasing anything that was in Britz's possession, nothing!" He realized someone was tapping gently but firmly on his bedroom door. "I have to go. Britz's mother arrived yesterday. I'm wanted."

Emily was talking again as he pushed the lever on the phone cradle down to end the call.

Where would she have stashed those papers? Obviously nowhere in the bedroom they had been sharing. She never worked in here....

"Max!"

It was Theo at the door, holding a grey legal-size envelope. "Look what that bastard Burton has done!"

"Help me find the papers Britz brought home from Dawson!"

"His lawyer is filing a formal complaint with Wellington-Weeks."

"Weeks?" Max was fumbling at a bureau drawer holding Britz's socks and tee shirts, but not Dawson materials.

"My *publisher*!"

"We can deal with them, tomorrow, Theo. Tomorrow. I've got to find Britz's papers. Now. Today."

"I never called them or my agent. Britz said I should. So did you."

'Where is your mother right now?"

"I ordered some food for her. She's at the kitchen table."

"So keep her occupied while I'm looking. Unless you have an idea where she'd have put them."

"In the baking dishes. Probably behind the big bag of flour."

"See if you're right." Max was back on the phone, looking for a messenger service that would answer a call from Vinegar Hill.

§

Theo was right. The envelope Miller had given Britz was there in the back of a bottom cupboard, along with the two floppy disks and material from the pharmaceutical firm. Max was right too. No one was going to make a pick-up. Not that far west on depopulated Hudson Avenue for someone who wasn't already a client. He got gibberish or runarounds from every downtown messenger service he called. Probably think it's a drug deal or some damn prank, he muttered to himself.

All the while he was calling messengers he kept hearing clicks on the phone indicating someone was calling or trying to record a message for him. The phone rang again almost as soon as he ended his last call. He switched the answer function to mute so he wouldn't have to hear. He'd have to walk over to Gold in the darkening afternoon. It was dark this early he realized because it had begun to rain, turning what was left of the snow into grey slush everywhere. Oh great.

"Mrs. Henneberg," Max began, once again seeing Britz herself calmly eating egg and bagel at their big table.

"My dear Max, it's Effa. Spelled A o i f e. But just the same. Please." Even her smile is the same, Max thought as his stomach cramped.

"I have an errand I have to do. Sorry to run out."

"Theo and I will make a dinner," she said without smiling.

"Please don't answer the phone or the door while I'm gone, Effa. You either, Theo. I'm not sure what's in the house to eat at this point. I can call later and bring something back."

"We'll improvise," she said, wiping crumbs from the corner of her mouth and ending it.

"Right. Best not to go out."

BRITZ LEAVES SOME POINTERS

It was pouring cold rain and Max realized he had never looked at the Dawson print-out for any sign of Britz. Scribbles in the margins, folded corners, slips of paper. He couldn't stop to do it now; the rain was slanting, he had a long walk ahead, plus he hadn't called Conner back to let him know he was coming right now so he had no idea if he'd be stonewalled at the precinct. He had even less certainty about when he and Conner could talk the whole business through.

On the other hand, despite the fact that below his knees his pants had began absorbing rainwater, it was far better to have all the stuff Theo had retrieved from the kitchen cupboard in police hands. He'd wrapped print-out, disks, and even the pharma promotion stuff in bubble wrap and stuffed it into a backpack. It was beyond good sense to try carrying Britz's computer. There was a box with a screen monitor, a separate keyboard, and a tower into which disks could be inserted. Plus various plugs, wires, and chargers. Fifty or sixty pounds at the best.

Plus a not very water-proof backpack, he grunted to himself, picking up his pace and wondering how quickly

Miller and the Dawson Center could get that court order. "Don't answer the door!" his inside voice reminded the Hennebergs. "I'll call you when I get to Gold Street." At least his socks were thick wool, at least his boots had been leak-proofed. God damn, a taxi would be terrific.

Not a chance. Vinegar Hill was no man's land. . . between the old left-behind Federal houses, odd commercial shops and storehouses, there was mostly nothing. Just empty lots until he reached the city housing project with its looming dirt-stained brick towers, surrounded by untended segments of trash-strewn slush and a large faded billboard, "Welcome to Farragut Housing."

Well damn the torpedoes, Max laughed at himself. I wanted a place off the beaten track. I put myself here.

Myrtle Avenue with cheap liquor stores, fast food joints, and discount clothing outlets was positively warm and welcoming territory. Well, not warm. A rising wind was throwing gusts of icy rain in his face as he crossed and headed down Gold.

Conner was waiting for him.

They soon discovered that Britz's printout was indeed notated all over in her swift light hand. Like a palimpsest. Question marks, circles, arrows, with "see page 3A" and similar instructions. The only marking that made any actual sense to Max was a note: "Call Shahid. Early stroke dx?" Had she done so? Supposedly no one knew about her special assignment except Dr. Miller.

"Someone should ask him," Max said, explaining Shahid Patel's role at the lab to Conner. "You, I think."

Conner didn't reply. He was monkeying around with the disks, inserting one of them into the department computer. "No go. I don't know if it's the program or her password. Some people keep all their passwords in one file," he said, and then sighing, "Shit, I'm no computer guru. I think we'll need a search warrant to go further. Would her brother sign an okay?"

"Just fishing?"

"Pretty much." Then Conner looked up, guarded. "You know I got a call from my captain about this. Seems Richard Genovich is quote, unquote concerned. These Dawson people run pretty deep."

"Richard Genovich? The Wall Street guy?"

"He's a donor to the Center and serves on one of their advisory boards. Big cheese."

Max flashed to back pages in the *New York Times* where he'd seen a party photo with R. O. Genovich in bold face in the caption. A bulky middle-aged male in a top-drawer tux surrounded by two women and another man in similar evening dress all glommed together for a society photographer. A lot of jewels and big smiles on the women. The page had caught his eye because the words Dawson Center were also in bold face.

"What's your boss asking you for?"

"The short version is clear this up. Fast. It's in the way of some important people. My captain wouldn't be in a position to ask why." Conner took a Tums from a pocket tin and began chewing thoughtfully.

"A clinical trial for a new treatment," Max told him slowly. "From what Britz wrote it looks as if she had some questions. Miller knows she had this stuff. He even said millions was at stake. I wish I knew more. I'd like to call Shahid myself. Millions of what."

"I'm driving you home, man. I need that Theo to sign me an okay. Then I can get her computer and take it over to our lab guys. That'll be our best bet for opening it. Plus we have her print-out. Should help, Max, should help."

"Look, I gotta get to a market for some groceries and I should call my place."

"Okay the first. Nix the phone call." Conner looked stern. "Well," he began after getting a cold glare from Max. "Just in case someone is monitoring your place, man. The less said on your phone the better."

Max felt a twinge. Jackass. My phone might have been tapped for days. Britz was killed for a reason. Max knew that; he had gnawed on it like a stubborn bone for what it might tell him about *who*. But he realized now, the meaning of her murder hadn't sunk all the way in. There was a *who*, a real person who might not be happy about Max and his doings.

There were lights on at his place. He realized that warm light was spilling out of his big windows while so much else in the neighborhood was unlit, and empty. A sign someone's home. Theo. Effa. He was glad he'd never cut windows on the street side. It would be hard to see much from the street, or even from the parking area in front of his door. But light, indicating occupancy, would be gleaming. Light, reflecting on puddles in the front lot. The rain had tapered off and a dark pink city glow radiated off the low hanging clouds.

EXCHANGE

Only Effa was there when Max and Conner arrived.

"Theo?" Max asked.

"He was getting quite intense about the threat from those neighbors," Effa said. "I couldn't ask him to wait here for you. I think he went into the city to see his agent. Something like that. Or he might have gone back to his own place."

She had cleaned up the kitchen and now set out glasses for wine. Something smelled delicious. Max set his brown paper grocery bag down and stomped off to his bedroom to change his shoes, his soggy work pants, his soaked socks.

"Way, wait, Brady," he called from his room. "Ms. Henneberg is Britz's mother. Can't she sign whatever it is you need?"

"Good enough," Conner yelled back. "I want our techs to open your daughter's computer," he explained to her. He yanked out his notebook and extracted a form for her.

"Can't you do more? What about anyone who can understand that printout and get what Britz might have had in mind?" Max asked from his bedroom.

"Not on P.D. staff time. Not unless we get some hard proof," he yelled back.

'I don't get you," Max said walking out to join them.

"Your forensic experts say she was hit hard on the back of her head. She didn't do it herself. You have proof!"

"Max. Look. We don't have suspects. We don't have a witness. We don't have a motive. We don't have one damn thing to warrant opening a *murder* case. We got 'suspicious circumstances.' Period."

"You do have motive." Max insisted. "Millions, remember. Money in millions, that's always a motive."

"So's her handbag. Which we haven't found. She could of met up with a bag grabber just going for a possible five spot. Zip to do with Dawson or any frigging million-dollar trial."

Max slumped into a kitchen chair and put his palms against his burning eyes.

"Or," Conner persisted, "this may have to do with the two fags across the street. Did Theo really steal that guy's book?"

"No," Effa announced.

"Do you know anything?" Max asked her very softly. "I mean has Theo spoken about it to you?"

"He doesn't need to. Nexfield was his spirit guide."

Oh for crying out loud, Max's mind ran. All I need is a half-baked spook. He tried to take her hand but she gently withdrew it, and placed both of her hands in her own accommodating lap.

"Well," Max turned back to Conner, "those guys are raising a stink but I'm betting they're on thin ice. They have a sample of Nexfield's writing *they* think shows Theo's book is really his. But ya know, influence in art is way damn sticky. Theo was his student and he sure was taken by the guy's work. Stands to reason *influence* got into his book. He's still a young writer. But they'd have to find consistent usage, exact same phrases. Stuff like that. It just won't happen." (I better pray not, Max thought.)

Conner was on his knees disconnecting Britz's monitor, keyboard, and standing drive. When he stood up he looked a bit bored.

"Would you like to stay for supper?" Effa proposed.

"I hope none of you need this thing for anything," Conner temporized.

"I hear I'm supposed to learn e-mail," Max replied. "Am supposed to if I listen to the Quorod Gallery. I like the telephone."

"Don't worry, man. Most of those guys are due for another interview. Higher-ups are on your side. Got any wrapping? Some old newspapers?" Max got tape and a roll of bubblewrap from his studio. The place felt both relieved and a bit too empty once Conner had taken all the equipment out to his car and driven away.

§

"You know Theo got a great deal from James Nexfield," Effa said over their supper. "It was symbiotic. They were meant to connect and did so intensely, after Nexfield's death."

Max raised his eyebrows and went on eating.

"I mean it, "Effa continued.

"You're telling me you know Theo had the missing manuscript aren't you?"

"Well, yes, " she said smiling. "He couldn't connect with the man himself after he was dead. He's no spiritualist. Neither am I." She grinned winningly.

"So you're saying he incorporated Nexfield's manu-script into his book?"

"It was deeper than that. He didn't copy words."

"I hope to hell not!" Max glared.

"The connection between them helped Theo break into parts of himself he hadn't had access to before. Nexfield was his *guide*."

Max was getting colder by the minute. "So from what you're saying it's obvious he lied to the police and everybody else, kept the man's property and incorporated it, 'symbiosis' as you put it. Sounds like any serious reader could see that. So he *can* be accused of publishing a book that isn't really his!"

"That's not what I'm saying." Effa was completely un-ruffled by his attack. "It happened during those weeks while he immersed himself in what Nexfield wrote. But Nexfield couldn't have written Theo's book. It's no more his than it's mine or yours. Something happened between the two of them."

"Did Theo tell you this?"

"In part," she admitted.

"What part? The part about taking Nexfield's pages and sneaking them out of his study? That he did tell me and Britz."

"Oh dear," Effa said with soft compassion. "Look, Max, if he hadn't taken what was given him he'd have been ignoring a great confluence. He would have deprived himself of a spirit-given opportunity to grow into the art-ist neither he or Nexfield could have been without this ex-change. It may hurt you to think he skirted a public truth, the police and all that, but he kept faith with himself and with his teacher. It was brave and true of him."

She leaned over his chair and kissed him, softly at first, and then with growing heat and urgency as Max was responding. He stood, turned toward her, taking in her intoxicating Britzness. Soon he had winnowed his hands under her dress. Her back was incredibly warm and supple. He steered them both to the nearest big couch and as she moved her hands under his shirt, freeing it from his pants and she moved a soft hand into his groin. He heard himself murmmer hoarsely, "Don't stop. Don't stop." He freed his belt. She scooped her lose dress up and over her head. Their tongues were twirling together in luxuriant exploration.

§

He came up for air on the floor among couch cushions and clothing in a tumbled mess. Effa's long bare body was lying full length on the couch just above him. It was actually morning. Grey light was streaming into the loft, brightening all the spaces. Insistent knocking at the door brought him to half-focus.

"Christ! The court order..." Max mumbled.

"Do you think?" Effa responded just as muddily.

"I'm too fucking old to sleep on the floor," he grumbled. He'd barely located and pulled on his work shirt when he realized it was Theo not process servers at his door. Theo was now loudly pleading, "Guys, it's cold out here!" while continuing to knock.

"Things do happen," Effa grinned, groping for her dress. "Better let him in." She gathered up her things and disappeared into the bathroom. Max pulled up his jeans and did.

Theo's all-important mission dissolved as he took in the scene. There was nothing to say. The muffled sound of the shower in Max's big bathroom ran as background while Max started coffee and began stacking a few of the deserted dinner dishes in the sink.

"Oh don't start washing up, Max!" Theo was struggling not to laugh at the sight of this large man fumbling with kitchen chores as if he could hang domestic respectability over the tumbled room. The smell of sex was everywhere.

"I've heard of this before, dear," Theo said.

"Well..."

"And so has she."

A hair dryer could now be heard from the bathroom.

"Well," Max rallied, "what's up with Wellington Weeks?"

"They've sent my manuscript and that little sample of James' to some specialist on plagiarism, but they don't seem worried. Not enough of James' work exists. Sadly enough. Everything's gone."

"Do you still have the pages you took?"

"I really wanted to keep all my early drafts. It's quite a trip, how the prose morphed. But after Burton and Eddy made that ugly fuss I just closed my eyes and put everything into the building incinerator. That was weeks ago."

"Who else has been in on this?"

Theo looked blank.

"You know nothing secret stays a secret. Every friend has a friend. I forgot the German for it, but my grandmother was a big one on the subject of gossip."

"You mean who's sharing in passing tales on me?" Theo fingered his hair. "I guess anybody. But what's the difference? If it makes me or the book a little notorious, what's to worry? There's already gossip about me making the rounds. Where did I come from? Am I gay or not? Who influenced Wellington Weeks to take me? Just wait, Max. They'll have me sleeping with the *New Yorker* woman as soon as her profile hits the streets."

A radiant Effa walked out of the shower, wrapped in a paisley shirt and a baggy pair of Max's shorts.

"Sleeping with who?" she asked Theo.

"You should talk!"

She ignored him.

"We have work to do this morning, Max. I want you to walk me around the neighborhood. And Theo, don't come. Just the two of us will be quite enough."

Is there any point to which you would wish to draw
my attention?"
   'To the curious incident of the dog in the night-time."
   'The dog did nothing in the night-time."
   'That was the curious incident," remarked Sherlock
Holmes.
                    —Arthur Conan Doyle, *Silver Blaze*

TRANCE

The neighborhood seemed more quiet than usual. The
loudest sounds were when Max and Effa's boots hit
crunchy patches of frozen mud. Windows in Burton and
Eddy's place were shrouded in heavy brown velvet...cur-
tains from a defunct off-Broadway theater, Max remembered. Burton had been gleeful about obtaining them.

Max and Effa walked in uneasy silence up the bumpy
street toward the Mafia bar and luncheonette, which never opened until 11:30 or so. Effa stood on the top step of
its entrance, swaying a little. Her eyes were closed. She
spread her palms on the door and then moved them to
the doorframe.

What a major jackass I am, Max was thinking. Am I
so undone by Britz's death that I have to sleep with her
mother? Was I looking for a *daughter* in Britz? What kind
of creep am I? Or else such a sitting duck, all I need is a
pull on my pud to forget everything? And now I need to
be thinking clearly, not following this spook-lady's wonderful cunt. Who took Britz? Who took her away from me
forever?

Effa began walking up the street, turning onto Evans, the narrow lane leading to the Admiral's House in the Brooklyn Navy Yard. Max followed leaving some twenty feet between them. The house itself, a beautiful Federal mansion, still owned by the U.S. Navy, but sealed and unoccupied for years, could be glimpsed only in sections. It was behind high brick walls. Effa stopped by a gate guarding a narrow driveway leading from the lane into the property and through which a lawn, big trees and half of the back of the building could be seen. She stood there as Max watched from the corner. Tears began rolling down her face. She knelt on the slate sidewalk in front of the driveway gate and lightly ran her hands across the flagstones, keening to herself.

Max waited. It took a while.

When she rejoined him at the corner her eyes were dry, her mouth tight, her face a burning red.

"The people in that luncheonette know something," she announced to him in a low voice. "But they're criminals and will only lie to the police. I think you can do something."

The "you" she'd said hung in the air. They walked back to Max's building in a silence she did not break until the evening.

Len says one steady pull more ought to do it.
He says the best way out is always through.
And I agree to that, or in so far
As that I can see no way out but through.
　　　　—Robert Frost, "A Servant to Servants"

PERSISTENCE

While Max and Effa were out the process server had indeed arrived. Despite Max's instruction, Theo had opened the door to stop the pounding and there it was. Theo was to present the print-out and floppy disks Britz had taken from Dawson Center to a courtroom in downtown Brooklyn or be in contempt of court. Britz's computer was not mentioned, but thermofax copies of the receipts Britz had signed were attached to the order. Conner told Theo he'd be over later to pick it all up. He said the court order wouldn't be valid as everything listed on it had already been placed in police hands as evidence in a suspicious death investigation.

"So tell Max to hold tight. We'll shove a lot of paper around, to make sure the dates click," Conner had promised. "Big buncha bull," was his conclusion.

Theo was bubbling with ideas about how to distract or humiliate Burton MacIlherny and he'd persuaded Dora to take a break from her endless labors, come out to Vinegar Hill and eat supper with the three of them. Neither Max nor Effa were much company. To their relief, Dora took Theo on, gently torpedoing every rococo scheme he described.

"You probably don't need to do that," was her kind refrain. And then she'd explain why.

Max realized the two of them were having a fine time with this. Effa, however, was impenetrable, remote as the moon. For his part, Max was visualizing the denizens of that luncheonette. There was Big Vinnie, he of the huge ball of money at whom Britz had once stared almost open-mouthed. Vinnie habitually sat at a table in the back and seemed to eat slowly but continuously. He had a large paper bag standing open at his feet. Pimps walked in and dropped their wads of cash there with barely any acknowledgement from him. Vinnie was all business. He was usually accompanied at this table by two or three sub-lieutenants, uniformly deferential and striving to be engaging. They dropped their voices or stopped their story-telling altogether whenever Max came in for take-out.

Up to this point, Max had never stayed long. He'd order a beer while waiting for hot food, or just watch while his hero was assembled. There were two regulars behind the counter: Tiny and Marty. The cook was Marty, a wired little athlete, who almost bounced from one kitchen chore to another. His deft hands were covered in luxuriant black hair and his fingers handled knives and spoons with delicate ease. Tiny was not much help. He was rangy, very tall, congenitally awkward, and almost always silent. He stayed out of Marty's way and handled beer, dishwashing, and the wrapping and packing up of take-outs. He clearly needed concentration to keep his elbows and knees from going in the wrong directions.

Except for the noonday parade of fancymen bringing deposits for Big Vinnie's paper bag, the place was rarely occupied. Nevertheless Marty cooked endlessly, provisioning events that were not in the neighborhood. Tiny would fill shopping bags full of delightfully fragrant foods and hand them off to men who often left their cars running when they ran in from the street. Max had never seen money change hands. Marty and Tiny offered casual "good to see ya," "say hi to so-and-so," "g'luck", or some other monosyllable and Marty would give or receive a high-five every once in a while. The food he cooked was on the whole fabulous. Rich tomato sauce simmered in a huge pot on a back burner, steam from pasta flew up, so did flames from his small iron frying pan. Marty chopped and flipped, mashed and maneuvered through all the standard South Italian classics.

You could watch a ballet, Max thought, and not see more acutely executed moves. All the while Tiny spoke hardly at all and Marty wasn't included in whatever was transpiring at Big Vinnie's back table. Maybe Effa had a point. He might talk to Max.

§

Max took off for the luncheonette the next afternoon, timing his visit for the gap between visits from cars the pimps used and cars that habitually stopped for food pickups much later in the afternoon. This gave him a morning for studio work. He needed to recover from the grief binging. He was trying to work though the grief still stolidly pounded on; he knew he needed to bring himself back into a more orderly focus if he was to avoid a deep hole of depression almost visibly threatening him. His main task.

Conner had been incommunicado ever since Max had urged him to re-interview Karl and Shahid at the Dawson lab. Just as well.

Max sat on a counter stool and drank his beer silently.

"I can't stand eating at home anymore," he said to Marty at last. "Either I hear myself chewing or I'm facing my girl's mother. She came here when Britz, um, well you know. When they found her."

"Britz?"

"M'girl's name." He returned to his beer. "Britz Henneberg," he said to his glass.

"Bummer," Marty responded. He didn't ask for details, which Max figured had all been thoroughly passed around. "Ya know Big Vinnie's damn upset about that," Marty said after a moment. "We all are. This is a quiet neighborhood." (Meaning, it was clear, this is *our* neighborhood and we don't like anything from outside disrupting it.)

"Mrs. Henneberg keeps wanting to make dinner. I don't know what to say to her. I mean the cops won't release her body and we're just in fuckin' limbo. I want a funeral, so the old biddy can go the hell home."

"Ya mean they don't know what happened?"

"Oh yeah, they said they told me everything. I can't get anything more out of 'em. Someone hit her on the back of the head. Hard enough to break a neck bone. Shit. It's like she's being killed over and over. 'Person or persons unknown.' Fucking hell." Marty was leaning on the counter opposite Max, in genuine sympathy.

"One thing is I'm not gonna let the old lady cook. I don't like watching her use Britz's pots and pans. Goddamn it. Ya got some of that veal parmigiana I can take out tonight?"

"Ya wanna bring her in here?" Marty asked.

"I'd love it but she won't go out. The neighborhood scares her. The city scares her. She's from boondocks, ya know, some place way out in Indiana. She just sits there. I can't stand it."

"I'll fix you up. Hey Tiny, pack up veal parm for two, put in some salad, loaf a bread. I make a killer tiramisu, yeah? Two a them, Tiny. In the fridge."

"Jesus, Marty. Saving m'life." Max dug out a twenty from his billfold and set it on the counter under his beer glass.

Two more beers and he learned Marty has a wife, a little girl and two boys, shares a house in Bensonhurst with his cousin's family, never leaves Brooklyn except for the Jersey shore weekends in the summer, and when he was drafted for Korea and got sent to cook for basic trainees on an army base in South Carolina.

"Better'n gettin shot at. But you can't believe the shit they made us make. Un-fuckin-believable."

It was after six when Max got back to his building. Theo had gone elsewhere. Effa had finished mending her poncho and turning the collar of one of Max's frayed work shirts. The answering machine coughed up: Strangleford had called. Conner Brady had called. Emily Transholm had called.

PERSEVERANCE

Transholm rambled on about the memorial being planned for the University Club. But something told Max she had other things on her mind. Had he heard anything from anybody? She tried asking him that three different ways, which he ducked each time. She's sure got ants up her snatch, he thought.

Strangleford was even more annoying. He had flown to New York and he'd consulted a lawyer about his rights, he told Max. Rights to what was unclear. Britz probably had some savings and would be due some kind of death benefit from Dawson's insurance policies. Money is what he means? What a shit.

"Fine by me," Max told him. "Listen. Do you want to come to the Center's memorial thing? It'll be wine and cheese, folks from her lab, and a bunch of administrators saying nice things. Not too long. I just heard they set a date."

"No. Not. Wouldn't feel right," Strangleford said. He had been told nothing legal can happen without a death certificate, meaning the cops have to sign off. It was costing him a lot to stay in New York, he let Max know. "This waiting is real tough on me," he mumbled. He was just crass enough to push Max on when the police would move. When he mentioned the police he almost said "They should fish or cut bait" but some remote better instinct apparently made him keep that unsaid.

"Do you want to be involved in where Britz is buried? That's going to cost something," Max pushed. "Hey, no?" he said to the silence on the other end of the line. "Maybe you want to speak to her mother? Mrs. Henneberg's right here."

Strangelford nearly choked in his haste to curtail the conversation.

"I thought not," Max said, hanging up.

Now it was time to phone Conner Brady, but Max decided not to. Whatever had or had not happened over at Dawson when Conner re-interviewed the lab staff didn't affect Max's current preoccupation: Had anyone at all out here on Hudson Avenue seen anything the night Britz disappeared?

The same time the next afternoon he returned to the luncheonette.

The atmosphere was unsettled, charged. Four men were crowded around Big Vinnie's table. All immediately silent when Max entered. Tiny dropped tableware as he unloaded the under-the-counter dishwasher, eliciting Big Vinnie to break the silence with vigorous cursing. Marty was all business. He did shovel Max a huge helping of lasagna onto a tinfoil pie plate but he clearly wanted him to split pronto. So Max paid and left.

"What's all this food?" Effa wanted to know.

"It's what you said. The luncheonette people know something."

"Well, the food is very nice," she said thoughtfully. "We can eat it every day."

"I'm gonna keep going back," he answered, and a lump in his chest softened. They spent the evening playing chess, then he turned off the phone and they listened to old Chet Baker records. She'd been damned hard for Max to beat. The next afternoon he returned to the luncheonette again.

"Hey, Max," Marty spoke as if the tension of the day before had never happened. "You know a lot of people. Ya ever heard your girl talk about a guy named Billington? Some damn name like Westfield something. Billington. A big shot at that cancer hospital. Where she worked?"

Where the hell did he get that, Max wondered as he assured Marty he'd check it out.

"Westfield Billington?" he repeated to Marty. "Sure sounds like a blue-blood name. Ever notice how those guys get their names from places? Westfield!"

Marty hadn't noticed but he laughed a little anyway.

"I was named after some German movie star, to please my grandmother. She was not too happy about my parents' marriage."

Marty laughed for real this time.

This time he took home a hearty dinner of pasta with tomato and smoked eggplant.

"This is *real* guinea food," Marty bragged. "This'll put hair on ya balls."

"Sure hope it won't work that way on Britz's old lady. She's one ball buster already."

Once at home he went through Britz's desk until he found the most current annual report from the Dawson Center.

"Effa, you've got a thing for vibrations," Max said. "Come look at these names for me." Sure enough, the Richard O. Genovich that Conner had asked about was a Dawson board member. So was a J. Westford Billington.

Effa bent over the brief small print bios of board members. "They're both involved in investment firms," she said. "Don't be glib about vibrations, Max. Common sense tells me most of these people are investors. Money men. And they might not be immune to temptations like advance knowledge of medical trial outcomes? You don't need vibrations to know what huge money is involved in developing new drugs. Especially for cancer." She gave Max one of her luminous smiles. "Always amazing how the very rich fear it. They can't buy their way out. They can't be safe by moving to a hillside spa way way off somewhere."

Her image sparked a flood of Max's own: the 13th century wealthy fleeing London during plague, bringing along their retinue and their belongings to country towns, including of course their imported furs which in turn often carried hidden colonies of plague-bearing fleas.

"Someone has been talking about Dawson Center board members in Vinnie's luncheonette," Effa said, putting the publication aside. Yep, Max thought. Smart lady. Probably *is* a bit of a psychic. No wonder she's so hard to beat at chess.

Honor. Whoever appeals to the law against his fellow man is either a fool or a coward. Whoever cannot take care of himself without that law is both. For a wounded man shall say to his assailant, "If I live, I will kill you. If I die, you are forgiven." Such is the rule of honor.

—from Wikiquote.org

OMERTA IS AND AIN'T

"Tell me something on the QT, Marty. Did you ever see Britz in here?" The luncheonette was unusually quiet this afternoon. Vinnie had sent Tiny out on an errand and then, unexpectedly, slowly arose from his extra wide seat and left the place, taking with him the two men who'd been sitting in the back. Max knew better than to ask why.

Marty looked a little white around the gills. He stopped his cooking chores and began to scrub his grill.

Max broke the silence. "I been checking up on that name you mentioned, Billington? He's an investor who does things for Dawson Center. I guess I was wondering if Britz knew him. She was always a little close mouthed you know. Kept pretty tight if you know what I mean. I mean I just found out she was married and she never said a word. It kinda gave me a turn."

"That sucks," Marty replied after a long pause. He was still turned away facing his grill, and took a long time wiping and inspecting it before he turned back toward Max and the rest of the room.

"Mind telling me where you heard his name?" Max pushed.

"I never said nothing to you," Marty announced firmly. "Never. Get me?"

Max knodded. There was another long silence.

Marty broke it: "She did come in here this one time, kind of late, and she brought this nigger kid in with her. This would not make Big Vinnie happy."

"A black guy?"

"Well, he might of been an A-rab or something. He wasn't real dark. Anyway, I told 'em the kitchen was closing."

He looked up guiltily. "We never let project people in here. You know." He went back to scrubbing his grill before he spoke again. "Max, I don't think it was anything. I mean it wasn't like she had a *date* or anything. There was someone else outside and they all left together."

Max put his forehead down on the counter. "I didn't know her long enough. But I miss her like there's a hole in me." His voice was gravelly with emotion. He wanted to press Marty a bit more about Billington but he needed to get out. She had been here. And so had Shahid. And someone else. Could have been Kurt.

"No food tonight. You never told me anything. See you," he muttered as he walked out.

Propelled by rage, he ran all the way to Myrtle Avenue before he regained enough control to go the long way around back to his building and phone Conner Brady.

"Can you do anything with this?" he demanded. "I'd bet on my grandma's grave that the 'nigger' is Shahid Patel. He's Pakistani. Britz's lab mate. Fer Chrissake can you find out if anyone called here from the Center that Thursday night? I'm sure you didn't get much out of Shahid or Kurt but don't you have a move now?" Max didn't stop to hear answers:

"And while I'm at it, when do you guys quite futzing around and let us have a decent send off for Britz? We want her cremated. We want you guys to stop poking around with her remains. It ain't decent. What's the goddamn problem?"

"One question at a time, man," Conner said. "First, we're holding all physical evidence for resolution. I'm sorry."

"You can damn well level with me about where you're at," Max answered, feeling Effa standing behind him listening intently.

"There's a lot of pressure about this. From higher-ups. What can I tell you? Dawson Center. Ya know what they say about the rich and famous."

"Rich and famous nothing. I'm telling you I can't give you shit for physical evidence, but I know Britz was killed right here on Evans Street. Those two, Patel and I think it's Ziek, Karl Ziek. They were here with her at ten-thirty that night. They did it or they're in on who did. Guy in the luncheonette saw them, but you know that place. That guy would never say."

Max could hear Conner sigh.

Max hit the dining room table with the side of his fist. "God damn it to hell. They carried her down to the river and threw her in. Threw her in like garbage. Your report had better be right. She didn't drown in that filthy water. Did she? Did she?"

"Hey, hey, the autopsy's tight on that. Her neck was snapped. Back of her head hit something hard. No water in her lungs. It would have been real fast, Max."

This news was not soothing, not compared to the finality of death. "So how do we get these bastards?" he demanded

"Uh. Look for the motive. Follow the money. You're not wrong, but we gotta make a case. Hang in, man." Max could hear Conner chewing. Man that guy eats a lot of those antacids, he thought. "We have some leads," Conner continued. "Please, hang in."

Max replaced the receiver on its cradle with elaborate care and looked up at Effa.

"What money," he growled at her. "He said follow the money. Britz didn't have money."

"It's that printout Britz was reviewing," Effa was ice cold. "There were facts buried there that threatened someone's plans. Take a breath, Max. I spent some time at the big Brooklyn library yesterday afternoon. It got to me when you wanted me to look at those board member names. I found an item in the *Washington Post* about an FDA advisory board meeting to review data on something called tissue plasminogen activator. It caught my eye because I think that's the same material discussed in Britz's papers. tPA. A possible treatment for stroke?"

Max grabbed the telephone and called Conner back.

"I'm okay. I'm sorry," he got out quickly, as soon as he heard Conner's voice. "I'm thinking about the lab boss, Dr. Miller. I don't know what he's said to you, but does any of it relate to a new stroke treatment called tPA?"

"That's a little above my pay grade, Max. But we do have him on the radar."

"God I hate that crappy slang. Radar! You mean you've got him under surveillance?"

"You know I can't tell you that. But I do know the Center is having a memorial, 5:30, this Wednesday. We'll have some eyes on it."

"I will too," Max said, clicking down the receiver for a fresh dial tone.

> Retaining walls are great when they work as designed.
> However, the forces of nature and laws of physics can
> work against even the best engineered retaining walls.
> These forces can cause catastrophic failure.
> —*The CSE Landscape Architect*

AND ANOTHER BREAK

Max wanted to be sure Theo was well prepped for the event at the Center and up on his own latest thinking too. It took a long time for the rings to be answered. Max had almost hung up. Theo's voice was distant, sounded squeezed, making Max wonder if something from MacIllerny and company had burgeoned out of nothing.

"It's Albin," Theo whispered, and then gathering energy: "Let me talk to my mother."

Effa took the phone, her face flushing more and more intensely as the call continued. She finally got a word in: "We'll deal with it Theo," she said. "Come on over to Max's. We should all be together."

Max waited for her to explain. Instead she went outside, coatless, and sat with her arms in her lap on the building's low stoop. Max wasn't sure if she were singing or chanting. He opened the door briefly to ask if she wanted her poncho. Then closed it quickly as she had simply shaken her head. When she finally came in she asked Max for candles. He gave her a box of plumber's whites and she proceeded to make a circle of them on one of Max's dinner plates, melting the bottom of each so it was affixed to the surface by a small layer of melted wax. She used seven of them. Max went into his studio and began spraying fixative on his recent charcoals. Before Theo arrived he'd set up and fixed a dozen of them, added names and numbers to the backs, and entered information into his graphics ledger. He pulled one drawing out of the lineup and destroyed it. He could smell candles burning down.

"It's my father," Theo said, as Max opened the door for him. "Effa, how in hell's name did Albin know?"

"Don't swear." Her voice was throaty and low. "She's his child, Theo. Just as you are. He would know."

"How did he find me?" Theo was urgent.

"Don't think for a minute he didn't know where you were, *ever*." Effa was louder now and icy.

"If he wants to be at Britz's memorial, his name has to be on their list," Max pointed out.

"Call them, would you?" she replied in a flat tone.

"First tell me straight, Effa. Is he dangerous?" Max answered.

She didn't respond.

"*Effa*, I mean it. Does he have a plan?" Still no answer. Max walked to his front door, turned around and leaned on it miming a blockade. "I can put up with this only so far. Can either of you tell me what you think this is all about?"

"She is his child, Max."

"That's why I'm asking. Personally I want to beat whoever did this to a bloody pulp. Is he feeling that way too? Is that what he's coming for?"

"I expect Albin's ideas about punishment are a bit more sophisticated," she chided. "More than that, well, I can't speak for him. Theo, did he tell you when he'd arrive?"

"No. And he was bloody arrogant. Look, I haven't had a father or a mother since I left Halcyon and I don't intend to have either of you now." He turned away from his mother and wrapped his arms around himself. It was a gesture he was using more and more often. "If you ask me, Max, I think he's come for money," Theo said suddenly. "News of my book travels. Look at that creep who claims Britz married him. He's sniffing for cash like a truffle hound. I think that's Burt and Eddy's problem too, no matter what they say about how much they just *loved* James. They'd like to get paid off by Wellington Weeks. You'd be surprised at what I've heard since my book came out."

Effa's face wrinkled, whether in distaste or disbelief was unclear; the tension broke because Max's landline began ringing. All three of them looked at the phone before Max put the receiver to his ear.

It was Ji-Yoo from the Dawson lab. One of the FDA advisers had informed Miller that the committee was almost certain to reject his tPA data. He'd been invited to offer the lab's rebuttal on Saturday if he so chose, but the outcome seemed certain. The decision would be formally announced on Monday. Ji-Yoo wanted Max to know this will not, will not, she insisted, interfere with the Wednesday afternoon memorial for Britz. Even though her lab was in turmoil.

"You can imagine. We start all over again," she told him, almost panting. Emotion from her was very rare. "This is a *good* molecule! But this means we rework everything and the pharma money may not stay with us."

"Gee," Max said with as much interest as he could muster, "I'm sorry to hear this. I know Britz and all of you had put in a lot of work. That assignment Britz had been given, the papers she was working on at home? Sounds as if that doesn't mean anything any more..." It meant even less to Max, posed against the loss of Britz's life.

"Dr. Miller gave exact same assignment to Karl and Shahid," she broke in sharply. "He does things like that. Everyone wasted time. Just makes me crazy!"

Max concluded with a few pleasantries and gave her the name Albin Henneberg for the guest list.

"He's Britz's father," he explained, "He's here from somewhere way in Central America."

§

"Well," Theo said. "I wonder how many of the Dawson fat cats have managed to dump their stock with that little bit of info? Hard to believe that Miller would have kept it to himself."

135

We believe that death is both a private and a public
matter. While the death of a family member is a very
personal loss, that death also effects distant family,
friends, and the community at large.
  —*The Purpose of a Funeral*, brochure from
Barton Family Funeral Service, Inc.

AT THE UNIVERSITY CLUB

Wednesday afternoon a number of friends gathered
at Max's place, unwilling or uncertain about arriving at the Dawson Center on their own. In fact the event
wasn't at Dawson proper, but just across the avenue at
the university club of Dawson's close partner, the august
Reagan University. Theo, Dora, Lois, Bill, Clipper, Rose
Ann, Beth and Four Stove had all arrived at Max's Brooklyn building in plenty of time to imbibe stimulants or re-
laxants and to reinforce their alliances. Most had never
met Effa and were clearly fascinated. She was paler than
was normal even for her, dressed in a soft black caftan
with two large half-moon earrings and seven silver rings.
There was one on every finger except her thumbs and her
left-hand forefinger. Each had a symbol for one of the solar system's planets etched into the front surface.

Max had called for two large car-service cars.

People were splitting up and climbing in when an exquisitely tailored white-haired man loped up the street.

"Effa, Theodore!" he commanded. He was wearing
what was clearly a Saville Row suit, handmade shoes,
and an open Burberry raincoat beautifully lined in tweed

wool. He had a small leather satchel on his shoulder and had obviously exited a taxi at the corner, which was now turning back up the street toward civilization.

"Albin?" Effa held her left hand up like a cop stopping traffic and he stopped his approach about six steps away from her.

Everyone from the second car stopped to stare at the man and Max could hear Theo's breathing, raspy and shallow. "Let's go," Max said and steered Theo toward the almost full first car, shoved him in, and told the driver to go. Then he put his arm around Effa's waist and inserted her into the front seat by the driver of the second car.

"This is Theo's father," he announced. "I'm afraid we're a bit late," he told the driver. Everyone else scrambled in, with Albin Henneberg folding himself expertly into the last open space in the back and Max wedging himself onto the jump seat.

There was nervous pushing and shoving.

"Are you going to speak?" Lois asked Max.

"No. This is about Britz's colleagues. People she worked with at the lab. I've asked them to leave me out of it."

"We ought to do something for the Britz *we* knew!" This from Bill, somewhat muffled by Clipper's huge duffle coat which had become wedged over part of his face.

Lois started to cry. "I swore I wouldn't," she snuffled, prying an old tissue from her pocketbook.

"Please," Max told her. "It's okay, but we all want to."

The large car rocked on over the bridge and through the web of crowded streets. Lois's tears had settled something for all of them. When they reached the Upper East Side, a quiet collection of sobered souls exited in front of the sign for the Reagan University Club. They were ushered to a table where their names were checked, to a cloakroom to be relieved of winter coats, and then into a large thickly carpeted clubroom where white coated waiters were already passing plates of small sandwiches, fried shrimp, and tiny pastries, all studded with long green toothpicks.

Low overstuffed leather chairs were set out in conversational groups and a white tablecloth covered a long side table, presided over by two other waiters dispensing liquors, wines, and fancy water. Most of the people were not sitting but were grouped in the large open space in front of a low platform where a lectern with a mike and a small light awaited the start of whatever the Center was offering as a program.

Most of Britz's lab mates were already there Max noted, and dressed as if for a church affair. Neckties, jackets! Not a single scrofulous t-shirt in sight. Had they come to work in the morning like this, he wondered, suddenly conscious of his usual garb—a well-worn green sweater pulled over a faded blue denim work shirt. Not that it bothered him. I have my uniform, he often said to himself.

Ji-yoo touched his elbow to introduce him to her very Westport appointed, very WASP husband. She was wearing a dark blue skirt. Max hadn't known she had a husband or a skirt. Husband grabbed Max's hand in a firm handshake, his blue eyes looking into his with impeccable solicitude.

"So sorry about your loss," the man said releasing his handshake and placing a warm hand on Max's upper arm.

Max skimmed the crowd before turning back to Ji-yoo. No Shahid. No Karl. Ji-yoo was holding her lips tight and flushing faintly despite her sternly controlled calm.

"Karl has disappeared," she told Max in a low voice. "We are told nothing about when or where he's gone. Since yesterday."

"Frankly I'm concerned about my wife's reputation," her husband said. It was a Virginia accent, not New England WASP at all.

Max turned toward him.

"I'm in research too," he explained. "For Dow Chemical. Ji and I have a pledge between us. No secrets. B'lieve me I know how easily the taint of unethical behavior can touch just about everyone."

"Unethical's a mighty soft word for murder," Max replied.

"Oh no, Bradley doesn't mean it that way," Ji-yoo began. "He's..."

"Is she here?" Max interrupted. He meant Emily Transholm. Max's scan of the room had not located her. He was also trying to spot Conner Brady's "eyes" whoever they were. Instead he caught Shahid Patel, who was moving quickly toward them.

"I need to tell you Dr. Miller gave me and Karl the same assignment as Britz," Shahid blurted before he was actually close enough for a quiet voice.

"Ji-yoo said," Max answered, noting the small beads of sweat on Shahid's upper lip. Shahid shifted uneasily, clearly still working on how to work this out. "What do you think that means?" Max demanded, wondering if Effa had seen him and what move she might make when she did. The moment broke as Dr. Miller and Emily Transholm entered from a door in the back of the room. Miller turned on the lectern light, tapped the mike, and began immediately. He'd taken off his white lab coat, and was dressed in a comfortably worn brown tweed suit.

It was like church. Thanks and platitudes delivered in a low almost sing-song voice. Compliments for the teamwork of the lab staff. A recounting of Britz's contributions to several projects. Praises for her diligence and sense of humor. Surprise expressed at her moments of scientific insight. "Occasional" he called them. He had no idea how patronizing he was being and he made no mention at all of the stroke studies or the new medication. He closed by removing the glasses he had used to follow his notes, telling the audience how pleased he was that Max, "Britz's significant other," was present, offering Theo and Effa special condolences, and inviting personal comments from anyone.

To Max's surprise grizzled old Gyuri Farkis came up first to speak of Britz's cheerful morning greetings. Winston, Ji-yoo, and several others followed, while Max did his best to turn off his hearing. He didn't want to listen to any of this and distracted himself with an image of his favorite chair in which he could doze.

Winston cornered him when the talking was finally done.

"What's happened to Karl?" he demanded.

"I haven't a clue. Do you know anything?"

Winston took a step back. "I'm not a fool," he said foolishly. "Stock prices."

"I have to look after Britz's mother," Max responded

trying not to reveal the disgust he felt. Cheap insider trading? Was it really that obvious? Through the thinning crowd he saw Effa in deep conversation with an elegantly dressed older woman. Everything about her, from her careful hairdo to her chaste onyx earrings and her low-heeled patent leather shoes said money and social position.

She was holding Effa's hand in two of hers.

"Who's that," he asked Theo in a low voice.

"Mildred Flowers," Theo answered. "A real bigwig here. On the board. Endows chairs. Big bucks, you better believe."

"And you know her how?"

"She's my patron," he giggled. "She gives to the library and a lot of places. She came to one of my book parties—and now my agent is doing something with her about libraries for me." He wrinkled up his eyes and went on watching the two women in conversation with something approaching alarm.

"And Britz knew her?" Max persisted.

Miller hadn't left. He swept past Max and Theo to greet Effa and Mrs. Flowers. He augmented his greeting with an air kiss on each of Mrs. Flowers' cheeks, followed by a theatrical taking of Effa's hands.

"I am so honored to meet Britz's mother," he was saying.

"Excuse me, doctor. I'm Britz's brother and I think it's damn weird not one person has mentioned she was *murdered*," Theo blurted out. "All I know is the cops have questioned nearly everyone here and so far there's no damn clue about what happened to her. Why not! Why NOT?"

Movement and conversation nearby froze. Except for Shahid Patel who aimed a black glare at Theo.

"How dare you bring such upset here!" he snarled.

Effa fixed Shahid in her ice-gray glare. "You are?" she demanded. "Don't bother. I know who you are."

"My dear," Mrs. Flowers said to Effa.

"And you know I do," Effa continued undeterred. She quickly re-took the old woman's hands. "We know these things, Mildred," she said softly, "But you are exempt. Protected. You have a blessing. You may depend on it." She touched the her cheek and then softly kissed it. "Max!" she called out. "We need to leave. Theo! Please take my arm. Doctor Miller, take care. Your position is quite rightly," she paused, "unsteady," she finished.

Theo who had continued staring hard at Patel broke. Silent tears rolled down his face.

"I needed her," he said to Max, ending his eye-lock on Patel.

"Me too," Max growled, putting his heavy arm across Theo's bony shoulders. "Please tell Conner Brady to call me," he called out loudly to no one in particular, as he started to guide his small clan to the door. He was stopped by Gyuri Farkis.

"I need to tell you something," the old security guard said. "Let me get you across the street. My people'll get you a cab. I need just one minute."

"Just wait for me a second," Max called out to the car he'd hired.

The strength of a nation derives from the integrity of the home.
—Attributed to Confucius

OTHER NETS

"Ya know Big Vinnie's luncheonette?" Farkis asked as soon as he'd secured the door between the lobby and its security guards and Max. They were standing in the stairwell leading down to security's sanctuary. "I been thinkin' a lot since I realized you and your girl lived right down the street from them." He stopped.

It was clear to Max that Farkis wasn't quite sure what he could say to Max, or how much. Max patted the old man's back. "Buncha wise guys in there," he told him reassuringly. "And they are burnt that Britz got hurt on their turf. I wouldn't want to mess with any of them."

"I feel bad," Farkis said redundantly. "Your Britz. She may have seen...well, see, Vinnie's got a boss who, well, see, our fleet sometimes contributes, uh, transportation. Their cars, our cars. Whatever. It's quiet-like. Pickups down here no one sees. Did she ever say?"

"No, nothing. She told me you'd spoken to her about the old country."

"Well yeah. We did. You know she looked just like my grandmother. I mean pictures of her when she was a girl? Loved that girl." His rheumy eyes were bright with unshed tears.

"These pickups? Docs from upstairs?"

"Ah no. Mostly no. Mostly old guys. Center big shots.

Some of them guys love a game or two. So they just need quiet." Farkis mopped his face with a clean white handkerchief.

"Do you think anyone saw Britz down there when parking their cars or whatever? Is that what you're saying?'

Relief flooded his face. "Yeah yeah," he said. "I mean those bastards. I mean we get a call from Joe the Engineer, he's Vinnie's cousin. He's like Vinnie's boss. So I always know what's what. I never let her get near. Believe me. I *never*. But. Those bastards. Be careful. Hear?"

He opened the security door and let Max back out into the lobby. Max's head was roaring with connections: high stake poker games, society top dogs, expensive cars with darkened windows zipping in and out of the Center's subterranean parking areas, Vinnie's shabby waterfront luncheonette, money, money, money, ever changing hands.

Was it this and not the tPA stock racket that had dealt his Britz her deadly encounter? Would anyone anywhere ever do for her anything that could faintly be called justice? He got into the waiting car with Effa and Theo. The rest of the gang had scattered, heading elsewhere, together or alone.

"What about Albin?" he asked. Theo punched Max on the arm.

"You wan a knuckle sandwhich?" he asked.

"One ad is worth more to a paper than forty editorials."

—Will Rogers

Newspapers speak

The telephone!

"What the hell is Nexfield doing in my kitchen!" Max bawled. "Theo!"

THE TELEPHONE!

"It's the telephone, Max," said Effa's groggy deep-sleep voice. She propped herself on an elbow, and shoved tangled hair out of her face. "Max! You've been dreaming. It's the phone, the real phone."

"What the fuck's going on?" Max replied, shoving sheets and blankets aside. And then, seeing Effa among the pillows, he said, "Oh," remembering his offer to sleep on the couch and not much more after that. He fumbled for the receiver on his bedside table and snarled hello.

"It's Emily Transholm here."

Why's she sounding so fuckin' British? Max thought, struggling for a bit of clarity.

"I am sorry to call you so early," she continued crisply. "Is Mr. Henneberg there? Albin, Britz's father?"

"No. He isn't. Not at all." Effa was suddenly wide awake, gesturing at him. "No, I'm not sure where he is," Max went on. "Some hotel uptown I think."

"The Stanhope," Effa mouthed. "What does she want?"

"What's this all about, Emily? Christ, it's not even six fucking thirty!"

"I *am* sorry. I take it you haven't seen the morning papers."

"*Papers*! Of course not."

"Full page ads in the *New York Times* and the *Herald Tribune*. I don't know about the *New York Post* or the *Wall Street Journal*, but my people are on the phone right now. Max! Page 3! Can't buy better placement. We need to speak with Mr. Henneberg immediately. It would be extremely important," she was gulping a little to make herself slow down, "important for him to pull the ads in all the later editions!"

"I'm not following you, Emily," Max insisted. "Please start at the beginning!"

"Where is Albin Henneberg!" She was almost shouting.

"You could call Theo, but they are not on the best of terms." Max didn't shout back. He was firmly cool and about to hang up.

"Wait," Effa told him. She leaned over and took the phone. "Miss Transholm, is it? This is Aoife - Effa - Henneberg. Albin told me he hopes to visit the Metropolitan Museum today, so I'd try the Stanhope Hotel if I were you. It's just across the street. Now tell us about the advertisements. Did Albin place them? What do they say?"

"BEE-elzebub!" Effa burst out to Max. "She hung up on me!"

"Ya couldn't charm her?" Max teased. "Can't say I'm shocked. We better get ourselves out and over to Myrtle or wherever we can get newspapers and some breakfast."

The ad was very professional. A photo of Britz graduating from college in Michigan. Her security photo from the Dawson Center. The Building Department's record shot of Max's place taken when the renovations were complete. A news photo of Dr. Miller accepting the Lasker Award.

A tabloid-style headline read "Justice for Britz Henneberg?" The black question mark seemed larger than the rest of the type. The text briefly outlined the discovery of her body on Sandy Hook, and the miserable list of dead-end searches, adding up to a semi-conclusion that a promising young Dawson Center scientist, was dead of a broken neck, clearly a suspicious death, and no answers yet as to why this had happened or who was responsible. The ad was signed John Albin Henneberg. It included what Max recognized as Conner Brady's personal phone number, with a plea to use it to convey any helpful information.

It was tough reading this in a public restaurant while waiting for their breakfast platters to be delivered.

"How the hell did Albin put all this together—and when?" Max asked.

"Dear Max. He and I have spent years on the craft. Knowledge. Practice. Concentration. You could call him magician—or witch. He wouldn't care what you called it." As she spoke she unwrapped sugar cubes from a bowl on the restaurant table and lined them up in an open square.

"Magic square for flying in a white cloud," Effa announced.

"Oh, cut it out," he snapped. "Since when did your hus... husband? Effa, are you and Albin married?"

"We've had a ceremony. I don't think we ever acquired a *license*." She ladled considerable scorn on this
last word. "But we birthed and raised two offspring. And
we've shared living quarters for most of, let's see, thir-
ty-two years? Should qualify us as 'common law' I suppose. Why?"

"Just so I know," Max shoved his scrambled eggs across
his plate and onto a slice of rye toast. "What I really wanted to know is where's all the money's coming from?"

"That's got me too," said Effa. "We believe, that is he
and I used to be together on this. Profoundly against gambling of any kind. I still am. That includes financial in-
struments. It's not just a matter of the greed. To gamble
is to insult cosmic energies." She'd put her fork and knife
together on her almost untouched plate. Max could see in
her eyes how dead serious she was, so he refrained from
giving her the mocking rebuttal that was surging up his
craw.

"It's ungodly," Effa continued slowly. "Lower-case g.
Gambling can tempt a person into invoking demonic forces."

"You think Albin has been playing with the devil?"

"I don't know. I don't know what he's using to get results or if he's undergone a conversion of some kind. It
wouldn't be the first time. I don't know what and I don't
know how long this will last."

"But right now he's on my side, Effa. And he may be
able to help. I want justice!"

§

When they returned to Vinegar Hill there was a message on the answering machine requesting the name of a funeral home to which Britz's remains could be sent. Her body was now formerly released to her family.

Max phoned Theo and left him a message with this news. He then phoned Conner Brady. No answer...so he recorded a message asking him to return his call at the end of the day. All the oxygen in the air was gone. Britz was gone. The walls seemed to be moving in on him.

"I've gotta get out of here," he told Effa. "I'm taking the truck." He meant the battered brown and pink pick-up parked forlornly in the lot fronting his building. He meant to drive out into New Jersey. He was thinking he might go as far as Great Swamp. See if any early spring birds have arrived. See if being way out there could help him breathe. Just a drive. Out and away.

"Would you first take me to the museum, the Metropolitan?" Effa asked.

A MEET-UP AT THE MET

It was a long drive. Max's pick-up had seen better days. It coughed and clanked across the Brooklyn Bridge, and responded sulkily to the stop-and-then-go of traffic that clogged downtown streets leading to the multiple detours that had been put into service to replace what used to be the elevated West Side Highway.

"They never maintained it," he explained to Effa. "It was a dingbat design from the start. Too narrow, horrible curves. For twenty years everyone argued and stalled and the city spent no money on maintenance. None! Road salt. Heavy trucks. They had the last word."

"It collapsed?"

"A big chunk of it. But the city knew the jig was up so they closed the whole damned thing. The collapse could have been way worse. No one was killed. So now maybe they'll build this Westway thing, and maybe they won't. It's been a few years and all different groups push their favored idea. Put it underground. Put it overground. Stick it out in the river. You can bet the big time developers are biding time, drooling for prime riverside properties."

They'd barely gone three blocks in ten minutes.

"God damn. Why'd I go west any way. Should have gone up the FDR."

"Don't worry, Max. The museum'll still be there when we get there."

"You know we should talk about where *we're* getting." Max found himself jammed behind a large delivery truck and hemmed in from behind by an empty school bus. Behind them, drivers he couldn't see were leaning on their horns.

"Where do you want to go, Max?"

"I have to go on," he said. "On. That's all I know. You know you're so like your daughter it's really fucking with my head."

"I'm not her, not even close. But I am much closer to your age than you were to her's."

"I'm fifty-two," Max said. The truck in front took a hard left up Greenwich Avenue and Max followed. Tick-tock his head said. Halfway to what? On to where? When will I stop thinking about Britz all the time? Pain throbbed and danced across his belly and groin.

"Shh-IT," he roared as a heavy maroon Buick with fender ornaments like little bombs cut him off. "That's who I serve," he muttered.

Effa put her hand lightly on his forearm.

"Who else do ya think buys the art at Quorod's? Nice simple folks with second-hand Fords?" Max snapped.

"I'm fifty-seven. But it's not about our ages. No way are we to be a permanent couple," Effa said. "We need each other for now. We share a huge grief. I think it's okay."

"I don't." He looked at her. "But of course I do," he

admitted after a pause. He had put his hand between her legs. Then yanked it away from the wonderful warm for a quick two-handed manoeuver around a huge Sanitation truck and a dark blue sedan whose driver gave him the finger as he passed.

§

It was almost three-thirty when he pulled into the Met's underground parking lot and fished for the cash from his wallet. "Any particular place?" he asked her. He knew she was looking for Albin.

She wanted to get out from underground and walk in the daylight up the museum's majestic front steps. It was still windy but the sky had brightened. Bare trees were tossing in the park across the street, with a few of them, willows for sure, showing an early spring haze of light yellow.

"So what do you know about curses," he asked Effa as they went up the steps.

"Cut it out!" she snapped back. "Black magic is ungodly. And just as likely to bounce back on you. It's not a joke."

He thought she'd want to visit one of the more occult places, the Egyptian collection or maybe the Middle Eastern rooms. He followed her as she went up the wide interior stairway. She apparently needed no directions but moved purposefully through room after room until they reached Northern Europe, seventeenth century, and the Rembrandts. She stopped in front of "Portrait of a Young Woman with a Fan" and returned the painted woman's

152

direct regard with her own even gaze. Max was more taken with the lush white lace cuffs and neckpiece, clearly painted rapidly and with exciting dexterity—just enough for a full suggestion but with no excess, set starkly against an opulent black dress. He was jerked out of his concentration by Effa's sudden move.

"Theo!" she said sharply.

"Dad's here," Theo replied from the entranceway, pushing his long hair away from his eyes and tucking it behind his ears. "Did you follow him?"

Sure enough not only was Theo walking in but someone else was now in the room that had previously been empty. A tall man in an expensive raincoat was bending over to view up close a Rembrandt etching of a small country house set among trees. Max gave Effa a swift pat on her back and strode over, putting his hand on the man's shoulder. Albin didn't seem shocked; he simply straightened up and looked into Max's eyes.

"I'm Max again..."

Albin cut him off. "Of course you are."

Max continued firmly: "I think you know I am as interested as you in finding the, the, the perps who did this to Britz. So—I want to know what you're doing in here. And I have some information to share with you unless you already know everything." To his dismay he could feel his face going red.

"I'm looking at an etching belonging to the Westford Billington family. It's on permanent loan. No doubt to cement a promised legacy gift." Albin stood back from the small framed image and stretched out his hands, fingers up, making a slow circle over the artwork, well outside the distance that would cause a security buzzer to sound. He sighed and turned back to Max.

"I thought he might have touched it. To be sure I needed to be near. " Albin's eyes narrowed. "He's quite the art lover, old Westie. So, what information do you have for me?"

"What is Billington to Britz?" Max could feel his red face starting to burn.

"More accurately, what is Britz to Billington?" Albin replied sharply and promptly answered his own question. "An obstacle. Only an obstacle. I don't believe he ever met her personally."

"I think I know that part, an obstacle regarding tPA, right? But how did he know about Britz's fact checking? How do you know about it?"

"I've been in contact with Dick Genovich. Richard O. Actually not him. I called his home but he's been in Europe for the six weeks. Treatment for cancer. I had a nice long chat with Isabelle, his wife."

"So glad to hear you could have a nice chat with Mrs. Genovich. That doesn't tell me how any of them got Britz's name, or if they ever had it!" By now even Max's ears were scarlet and stinging with frustration. How can I get a handle on this guy?

"Oh," was Albin's only response. But a very faint flush rose up his neck.

"How do you know these people anyway?" Max pressed. "We can't help each other if you go on being evasive." He waited, but again Albin said nothing. "Right now I'm asking about Billington and some, uh, 'special' card games." Max waited again.

Effa and Theo waited too. The two of them were standing together just across the exhibition room which was otherwise empty.

Albin spoke slowly. "Before I met Effa I had another life. We met when I was only twenty, but nevertheless. And I told her a very different story about myself."

Effa walked across the room to hear better. Her face was stoic, but her cool grey eyes were hard and oddly shining. Albin gave her a charmingly noncommittal smile.

"I took most of my biography from my sophomore roommate. He'd grown up in Danville, Kentucky and told me about the religious school there," he told her.

"Roommate where?" Effa demanded.

"Groton. Groton, Massachusetts, not Connecticut. The prep school. I was a student there until I was expelled."

"Groton! So your family must have had a fair bit of money," Effa said, catching on. "You were a privileged kid. So much for your hardscrabble Kentucky childhood."

"Fraid so. I was no scholarship kid. I've told a lot of lies in my life, my dearest. You were part of many of them. We were free, we said, and we lived it. We could declare new realities as we needed, remember?"

"I wish I could declare a bench in here." Effa said, rocking a little and leaning on Theo's arm who was now next to her.

"I'm waiting for information about you and Westford Billington," Max broke in. "Mister whatever your name is!"

"I haven't seen him since I was seventeen," Albin answered. "I have a different name, a different persona, even a different body now. In addition, I was expelled, a taint he would be unlikely to overlook. But I do know men like Billington cherish their schoolboy nicknames so it's a good bet he's still called Westie by his pals."

"I need to know if he's a player," Max was not going to be distracted. "Look, I don't give a rat's ass about the games *you* play. I want to know about him. I'm going to find out who killed Britz. And why. That's it."

"But I do give a rat's ass," Theo interjected and fixed Albin with a razor-sharp glare. "My mother and I both do. There's a whole scene here and it looks as if she and I and Britz, all of us, were played."

A school group was heading through "Northern Europe, Sixteenth Century" and a teacherly voice could be heard droning on about northern light and the differences between the Italian Renaissance and the Northern one. The group had paused in the adjoining room.

"They'll be in here in a minute. I think we should talk in the park. Even though it's cold." Max said taking Effa's other arm and heading for the main stairs.

"Much more comfortable at my hotel," Albin said. "It's just across Fifth from here. Look," he explained, "my hotel has a nice lobby. Small but we can talk privately as long as no one shouts."

Afternoon tea was introduced in England by Anna, the seventh Duchess of Bedford, in the year 1840. The Duchess would become hungry around four o'clock in the afternoon. The evening meal in her household was served fashionably late at eight o'clock, thus leaving a long period of time between lunch and dinner. The Duchess asked that a tray of tea, bread and butter and cake be brought to her room during the late afternoon. This became a habit of hers and she began inviting friends to join her.

—Historic UK.com

At the Stanhope

Albin ordered tea, a pot of which was duly provided on a large tray, complete with an extra pitcher of hot water, sugar, milk, and lemon wedges as well as sufficient cups and saucers. Albin was the only one who drank any. Everyone settled into the club chairs surrounding a small serving table but the atmosphere was hardly comfortable. Theo glared at Albin. Effa retreated into an icy clarity clearly to mask her emotions and Max, determined to enlist Albin in his search for Britz's killers, waited grimly. As Albin had predicted, the lobby was small but they were occupying a corner and weren't near the few other patrons. Some soft cocktail music was being piped in.

"Well," Max began. "Cards. Is your old friend a player?"

"Does he frequent private high-stakes games? Is that what you're asking? I wouldn't be surprised. As I've said, I haven't seen him since we were both seventeen and I don't think I ever played poker with him. But I do remember he liked a good dare, and he always relished situations he could win."

"Okay. Tell me, why are you talking about him now? And looking at a picture he owned?" Max was taller than Albin but he'd ceded his position as the lobby was Albin's turf. He didn't want to cede anything else.

"Yes, it is Britz as you surmise. A few Dawson Center board members stand to profit substantially from their stock in a pharma that will scale up this new medication. Billington's one of them." Albin's replies were meticulous and impersonal. His body seemed unguarded as if he were telling the truth, but Max guessed he was good at disguise.

"Did he know Britz?"

"No."

"So?"

"There's an adept on the Dawson board, low grade but an old and dear acquaintance of mine, Margaret Flowers. I believe you met her at the memorial. I know Effa spoke to her."

"Adept?" Max asked. "Adept at what?"

Albin gave Max a pitying look and continued.

"She and I had a few moments together and she filled me in on Dr. Miller, Britz's boss, and on three board members all of whom have been, well, affected by recent developments."

"I'm not sure what you mean but I've uncovered another connection to Dawson," Max said. "A luncheonette in my Vinegar Hill neighborhood. It's a liaison point for players who leave their cars and their regular drivers at

Dawson for private transportation. Britz could very possibly have seen or been seen by people in the Dawson garage."

"And that would be incriminating?" Albin didn't sound convinced.

"A mob-connected game, very concerned about players' privacy? I'm not sure how deep all of it goes. But here's how it adds up to me right now. I see two possible things to question. In that luncheonette and at the Dawson garage. But we don't have a shred of actual evidence connecting either to Britz's murder. We sure have people who aren't going to admit anything to anybody. Not Miller certainly. Not those board members. And not the workers either: There's a luncheonette employee deep connected to mob people. And a lab staffer who knows there's a problem with the tPA trials. He's the most interesting as he was seen at the luncheonette the night she disappeared."

"The night she died," Effa interrupted. She was taking everything in and slender cords in her neck were standing out. Max was too far away to touch her. He nodded at her slowly. "They were all there," he confirmed.

He turned back to Albin. "Talking could get that luncheonette guy killed. Talking would ruin the lab guy's standing, threaten his fellowship, his Green Card, whatever. He's a foreign national."

Albin listened sipping his tea.

Max continued: "Someone else was with the lab guy that night, I was told. Someone who waited outside. We have only a guess that he might be the other lab guy, the one who's now gone missing. But it might be someone else altogether."

"Okay, Albin," Theo broke in, his anger beginning to boil over again. "Enough games. Where does all the money come from?"

"Money?"

"*Your* money. Those clothes. This hotel. Everything!"

Albin was weighing his reply.

"I mean it, you monster. Pretty cool of you to care so much for Britz now she's dead. You had her locked up in a fucking nut house. God knows why she didn't actually go crazy. You told me so many lies when I was a kid I don't know why *I* didn't go crazy. Now my mother thinks you've been using something, second sight maybe, to make money gambling. I think you're despicable no matter what the reason." Theo's spit was flying and he was half out of his chair.

"Theo!" Effa put her hand on Theo's leg.

"Where's the money from!" His voice went down, not up. He almost rumbled.

"The family," Albin answered.

Effa and Theo said "No!" at the same moment, she in horror, he in fury.

Max stood up: "Hold on you two. This has to be for later. Right now is right now." He too glared at Albin: "Who can be induced to talk about what happened to Britz?"

Albin poured himself another cup of tea. Added lemon and stirred his cup.

Max was about to start again when Albin looked up at Max. "Tell me about the two we know."

"Marty is the cook at the luncheonette. Connected by marriage and I don't know what else, family bonds for sure. I don't know the name of the family. Wouldn't be hard to find out. And Patel, Shahid Patel, from the lab. Pakistani. He's here on some kind of fellowship. I don't know who from if that matters but he is totally focused on achievement. Very eager to please anyone if that will help him. Okay?"

Albin wasn't finished: "And what about the cops? Where are they in this?"

Max remembered he'd asked Connor Brady to call him back the night before but no call had come. "I'll have to check with my source," he said. "But they must have come to some fork in the road. They've released Britz's body. So whatever forensics they did are done. You know," he recognized suddenly, "Theo is next of kin per the police. He's the one who has to tell them where to send her body. "

"Oh good god," Theo wailed. "Am I spared nothing? I want her *in* her body. I want to turn it all back!" Max could sense Theo shaking again.

"Theo!" Effa said, "Control yourself. Arrange a cremation. Britz is not what remains. No more. You know that." She stood up to hold his shoulders. "As soon as it's done we won't have to think about the body we loved being filled with chemicals, probed by strangers. Please! We want her released. Her spirit freed."

Theo ignored his mother's arms and wrapped his own arms around himself. Tears were trembling on his eyelashes but he blinked them back.

"Patel, the Pakistani," Albin announced. "The weak link," he added addressing the ring of faces around him.

I'm the Romani rai
I'm the true didikai
My home is a mansion beneath the blue sky
I live in tent, and I don't pay no rent
and that's why they calls me the Romani rai
—Traditional Irish Travelers song

HENNEBERG WHO?

"Too bad he's not Catholic," Theo said icily.

"What?" came from Max.

"I'm ashamed of you," Came out of Effa.

"He might be," from Albin. They all spoke together.

"Oh Christ, Mozart does this sort of thing better," Albin added when they all stopped speaking over each other. "Catholic I suppose because of the love of confession?" he said to Theo. "Shame I think because you and I raised our children to think past categories," he said to Effa. "And *might* because he might well be. Many Pakistanis are Christian. Keep your stereotypes out of our way," he announced to the whole table. He rounded off his summary by stretching fingers on the tea table one at a time.

"You sanctimonious shit head," Theo replied as full of rage as before. "What's this family remark you made? What family?"

"Mine," said Albin. "And yours. Not Effa. She's your kin but she's not mine." He was signaling a waiter in the far distance, clearly seeking the check for the barely consumed tea.

"Hold on, Albin. You can't stop like that. What family?" Effa said.

"It's not Henneberg," he answered. "Ah, but Theo's right. There is money. Quite a lot of it. And a long story, covering many places."

Effa put her hands over her eyes. "This is a bit much. I think I want...I need to go home now." She suddenly looked shocklingly both old and grey.

"Where exactly is that?" Albin asked with a spiky edge to his voice.

"I'll take her," Max fired at Albin. "Probably best for you and Theo to talk. As you say, Effa's not in the mix. Nor am I." They did not shake hands or give each other any parting words but Effa did hug Theo briefly promising to talk to him later. She and Max made their way back to the Met parking garage.

"Not Danziger. Not Thurston. Not Hargrave," she muttered as she walked. She looked up at Max. "We used all these names in various places. I've told you we moved often. It always seemed either easy or wise. A change of persona. A different community. Different spiritual approaches. We went in and we went out. Albin used to say to us it's all about learning. But I always believed we were really Henneberg. That's the name that came first and we went back to it again and again. Henneberg. Now he says he just lifted that name along with a back story from some prep school roommate. Should I believe that?"

"You could think of adopting a new name just for you," Max said. "Or returning to the original name of your mother. What was it?"

She made no attempt to answer. They rode in silence. For most of the drive she seemed to be in some kind of trance. Unless she was sleeping.

"I need to talk to Conner Brady," was about all Max said as their silent drive back to Brooklyn was ending and he pulled up his pickup in the lot next to his building in Vinegar Hill.

The little black bird
asks for my heart
asking me soon to die
so I don't have to look at my children
　　　—Lyrics of "Oda kalo cirkloror" in *The Song Folk-lore of the Roma in the Slovak and Czech Republics*, 2016

ALBIN'S STORY

Theo's anger was unabated. He wanted to hit this infernal father of his. Smash his face in. At the same time, he wanted to run. To split, go far away, and never think of the man again. He had stormed out of the Stanhope and headed home, unable to shake how urgently he wanted to know what Albin had to say.

He crossed at 14th Street and took another subway back uptown. With all the time the train took, rumbling from station to station, conflicts roared inside him. He wanted the gaps filled, and at the same time he was sure he couldn't or wouldn't believe a word of it, no matter what the man who is supposed to be his father said. At the hotel he promptly used the house phone to demand that Albin return to the lobby.

"So you have a big tale to tell?" He cursed his father again. "Like who you are really. Like what you're doing really."

"Do you drink, Theo?"

"I'd like a taste of your blood. If you have any. No really," he switched up. "I'd like it to test whether you really are my father. Would be a great relief to get clear of you."

"You'd do better with a sample of my saliva these days. Have you heard about testing DNA? New thing. Just need a little bit of spit. Far more accurate than looking at blood types."

"Look, stop shitting me with your wah-wah erudition. Is that what I'm gonna get if I ask who the hell you are?"

"Whatever test you use you'll find that I am your actual father. No doubt. Don't you have a dark blue birthmark on the back of your neck?" Theo clenched his belly feeling that faint mark on his neck tingling. The Mongolian spot a biologist at Halcyon had called it, asking if Theo had Asian or African ancestors.

"Now, would you like a Scotch on the rocks? The bar in here has some pretty classy single malts."

"What happened to the Albin who favored plain water, room temperature? What happened to the Albin who bristled at the mention of class, not to speak of a disgusting term like classy?"

"Come on in here." Albin was at the open entrance to Gerrard's, the Stanhope's bar, all fitted out with dark green velvet sofas, dark wood over the bar, and more people than in the lobby. He led the way to one of the sofas. "I don't care who hears us, but I would prefer it if you refrained from blasphemies."

"Now there's a bit of the old Albin," Theo scoffed. "Just so you know, I wouldn't drink Scotch. You can order me a red pepper vodka. Put it on your tab and I'll listen to your big story."

And so he did.

"My name is indeed flexible." Albin began. "You've figured that out. The patriarch of our American branch was Florin Motsham Silvanis. My six times great-grandfather.

Your seven times. He was among a contingent of Roma men rounded up and ejected from France by Napoleon. They were shipped to Louisiana."

Albin accepted the two drinks being proffered on a small silver tray, pushing one across the service table toward his son.

"There was a labor shortage in French territories, a shortage of men to do jobs too risky for a slave. Slaves were worth a lot of money. Roma were trash. No one had paid for them, or invested in them, so they could be worked to death to no one's financial disadvantage."

Albin nursed his large single malt and crossed his long legs.

"Florin managed to run away. He ended up in Austin, Texas, where a small colony of other Romanis had established themselves. He and his descendants did well enough it seems. Lived in a shantytown, sure. Generations hung around together. Did the usual. Mending pots and pans. Cadging deals. And a whole lot of horse trading, horse breaking, horse training. Everyone in the family except my father had a passion for horses.

"My father broke with many Roma traditions, especially so when he married your grandmother. She was Gadjo. That means not Roma. She was actually Dutch. Maybe why you and **Godelieve** are so pale. A musician, she played only Western classical when they met. Even when I was little she could play European cello like a dream of heaven.

"She lit out of Amsterdam during the Great War. World War One. Even though the Netherlands was neutral she was being watched. Her teacher and most of the players in her chamber orchestra were German. And they'd toured all over Europe so they looked like possible spies. Arbitrary arrests were common. So were food shortages. It was definitely a place to leave. I don't know how the hell she ended up in Texas, but there they met. It might have been the practice that brought them together."

Albin was enjoying himself so much it was harder and harder to see this as history rather than fiction, Theo thought. His father had finished his drink and was signaling the waiter for another.

"The practice?" Theo asked, forgetting that he had promised himself not to react to anything the old man said.

"My father broke with the Romani order but he certainly kept to the practice. You'd probably call it gypsy witchcraft. He and your grandmother worked it together. She learned from him and she was a serious adept. Sometime in the 1930s, they settled in New England. By then she was using her cello to play Roma style. Nightclubs. Wedding parties. He got into used cars. That man loved machines like other Roma love horseflesh. He ended up with dealerships. New cars. Brighter the better. Made a huge pile. By the time I was a teenager I think he had more than fifty car dealerships all around New England. Passed himself off as Greek."

"Okay," Theo said. "So?"

"He died when I was 17. I was at Groton. He sent all six of us kids to expensive schools. Wanted us to be equipped for the WASPs, for high-class society, for politics, industry, the ruling class. My mother too. They were both into it. You bet I hated it. I didn't go home when they were told he'd died. I went questing. I sold my typewriter, all my fancy sports equipment, dressy clothes, books, emptied my checking account. I knew I needed constant movement to sharpen my skills, shake off all the materialist logic I'd been so heavily drilled in.

"So who would have what I needed? The Sufi? The Evangelicals? The Vouduns? I moved and moved. You remember some of it. I needed sex and that's where your mother came in. Effa, the dawn. Lovely woman." Albin smiled beatifically at his son.

"You selfish son of a bitch," Theo managed.

"I never saw my mother again. Seems she died about eight years ago. She stayed in New England and after a while my oldest brother took over the business. He died about six months ago. There is more than a billion dollars to split, the lawyers say, between me, my three sisters, another brother, and my dead brother's wife. I've been sent a retaining fee pending the final settlements. The lawyers do it all. "

"How did they find you?" Theo did it again. He couldn't help himself.

"The law firm put public notices in dozens and dozens of local newspapers, cryptic enough to keep the false replies down. Personally I think the family also sent some messages the witch way... and I'm not going to explain. There was a huge Roma funeral in Austin for my brother. Somewhere sometime there will be a huge funeral for your sister too..."

"Can they do that with just ashes?" Theo's curiosity was still flaring.

"Oh yes, as long as they can first burn her belongings and add her ashes to the fire.

Theo gave his father a stony appraisal. "If every word you've said is totally true," he said, "I still don't give a shit. I'm looking for a way to nail the people who killed my sister. That's all I want. All this stuff from you is just words."

"Words are your lifeblood, Theo. Don't speak lightly of words. Good lord you've become a writer, a keeper of words, a sender of words, a bender of words. You swim in the ocean of them and now they seep through you as if you had grown gills."

Supposin' I did kill the Black Dahlia. They can't prove it now. They can't talk to my secretary anymore because she's dead. They thought there was something fishy. Anyway, now they may have figured it out.
—Dr. George Hill Hodel, as recorded by the LAPD's "Black Dahlia" Task Force in 1950

Conner's findings

Conner, when Max reached him from his home phone was full-on Irish, unstoppably voluble.

"I hit the shit fountain for real," he bragged. "That Miller guy, the big-shot research doc? It didn't take much to get him spilling. He's way worried he might be tarred. Get that pretty white coat of his all smeared. Look, ya wana meet up at that Boro Hall bar again?"

"No. I'm just thinking it through," Max said thoughtfully.

Miller had given Britz the same assignment he gave to Patel and the missing guy, Karl. They were all in Miller's lab. I believe that part of it, Max was thinking. Miller wanted to be sure there were no flaws in documents the FDA was looking at. And there must have been some. My Britz got cast as the fixer. Because Miller knew she'd tell the truth no matter what it was. She'd zoom in on it and spot what else was wrong too. A lamb among wolves in that wonderful palace of cancer research!

"So spit out the rest, Conner!" Max demanded.

"You're right, Max. Miller told me he sent the two of them out to your place to pick up her documents. That night. Karl must a been the guy outside the luncheonette door."

"What about that creep. I mean Dr. Miller."

"Nah, Max. Miller says he planned to go over all the findings combined, one more time, and then take his concerns straight to the FDA. It was all on him, he told me. Okay, okay, maybe so, maybe not," Conner conceded, hearing Max's heavy breathing over the phone. "But you gotta admit he had a lot to lose and plenty of protection if he played straight.

"When Miller learned Britz was missing, I think he had a twenty-one gun shit-fit with the two of them. Karl and Patel. Scared 'em silly. He says they told him they never saw her that night and had to come back to the Center empty-handed. Which they were. That woulda have been Friday morning." Conner sounded palpably pleased with himself.

"So can you nail those two? Can you *do* anything? That little worm of a cook, Marty, he saw Britz with Patel. And he said someone else was just outside. God damn it!"

"Cold case file," Conner said slowly. "And that really bugs me, Max. It's anything but cold. We got a suspect on the run and another suspect shivvering in his pants. We could break this mother."

"Who says cold file it?"

"Brass. Who else? File and forget. Nothing conclusive. Yada yada yada. Ya know how many murders go cold case? Makes me sick how many. But this one, well I do wonder who put the muscle on shuttin it down."

"That's real helpful."

"We've really fucking got it." Conner was almost whining.

"Isn't it what you said, friend," Max answered. "Can't you follow the money?"

"Well that's another thing. Damn hard to prove unless there was an actual exchange of bucks." Conner let out something that sounded like half a belch and half a sigh. "I'm not expecting the brass to do any confessing. Or finking neither. They want this shut down. Period. Does seem kinda likely that some of those Dawson bigwigs, ones with skin in the game, would be real happy to have this matter in the deep six. Right? I think we're beat."

"Did you ask Miller about Karl? Where did he go and when?"

"I think Miller pushed him to run to tell you the truth. He was AWOL by Monday afternoon. By that time, Britz was officially missing and our team was doing search all around your place. But I didn't twig to Karl making a run for it until I went for the second set of interviews. Later. Let's see...I gotta check my date book."

"Don't bother," Max said, churning. "How does a cold case get reopened, anyway? Can you at least do an all-points on Karl?"

"Done that first week. Nothing. But I tell you that guy Patel is real scared. I see all the signs. Thing is now I can't lean on him. Case is on ice and I've been reassigned. I'm not a freelance ya know. I have a job. Shit, Max. I need to keep my jacket clean. That's what I was trying to tell you yesterday. I know this sucks."

Max's mind flipped, turned, sorting approaches. Could *he* speak to Patel? A woman, a mother, would be so much more likely to get to a guy like that. Would Effa do it? Would she wear a wire? A confession not recorded wouldn't help.

Conner laughed. "Jesus, Max. You been seeing too much TV. She wouldn't need a wire. This isn't 1940. You can buy a little recorder fits inside a pocketbook. They got ones that are voice activated. I'd want to coach her though. She'd have to get him to tell his story, she couldn't feed anything to him. That part's really not so easy."

"I wouldn't be shocked if she were a natural, Conner. This woman has a lot of sides. I'll have her talk to you before she sets up a meeting."

PACTS:
MAX & ALBIN, THEO & EFFA

"We need a war council," Effa announced as Theo entered Max's Vinegar Hill digs late morning the next day. "So I've asked Albin to join us."

She, Max and Albin had been drinking coffee when Theo rang the bell.

"There's a lot to digest," she continued.

Theo looked at each of them in turn, sat in a kitchen chair and folded his arms across his chest. His body language said "prove it." His face watchful.

"We need to concentrate on that 'weak link.'" Effa continued. "I mean Shahid Patel. It's quite straight forward, Theo. We'll never find evidence. There isn't any. We have to have a confession. Whatever Albin is or was is a distraction from that. We need to focus on what we can get: all four of us want some justice for Britz. We can not leave her death unredeemed."

"So why did you leave her in that dreadful place in Tennessee?"

"I can't make this better, Theo. We planned to get her out in a week or two, but things moved too fast."

"Meaning?" Theo was not moved.

"Meaning the local authorities were on us. Britz's transgressions were seen as our fault. I was really worried about the more hot-headed Evangels. A group of them came around one morning wanting to do some kind of exorcism on her. I thought getting her into the psych hospital would buy us a little time. She'd be safe from them.

"It wasn't just about our family you know. The locals were crazed about The Farm. It kept getting worse. The Farm kids could run around naked when the weather was hot. The scandal around Britz and God undermined every relationship we'd cultivated. Sam and others at The Farm were terrified. They could feel a mob with torches and pitchforks heading their way. And they were. We thought if we took a pass, things would calm down for them, but in the end, the poor souls lost their land and all the money and equipment they had. But we might have lost you both. There was talk of violence."

"Still you should have gone back for her!"

"Oh Theo, you're so naive. And so were we. The doctor we'd used to get her committed turned on us. Lied. The asylum records were altered. At one point they actually forwarded us a death certificate for her but we knew it was fake. That's the kind of cruel ploy they tried to smoke us out. Yes, we upped stakes. When we got to California, well, it wasn't a good idea to try to go back. We were, well. Well, I was persuaded that...our options were not good."

"You were always persuaded," Theo barked glaring at Albin. "You two never thought for a moment about *her*!"

"Stop there," Effa ordered. "We are not 'two' any more. Since that time Albin has strayed farther and farther from me and my beliefs. You must know what I think of gambling!"

"That doesn't make what you two did to Britz any better."

"It meant I had to disentangle myself. I had to do that hard work before I could do anything else."

"She thinks chance is anti-Christian," Albin injected. "Poor Effa. Up against greed and demonic forces, the influence of cosmology, all barriers to using occult pathways for attaining a pure soul."

"May the saints save you," Effa glared.

"I thought you were going to suggest Jesus," Albin mocked. "Look son, chance and risk—gambling always, gambling everything—that's what *you've* chosen to do. Haven't you? You're becoming an artist. What else is that? And you'll battle that drive against your need for a literary career all the rest of your unquiet life."

"Albin! Effa! Both of you stop." Max took Theo's coat and scarf and tossed it on one of the couches. "Stand down, everyone! You two can sort out your family drama on someone else's time. Right now we need to agree on our next step. In fact we've already agreed. It's Shahid Patel. I think Effa has the best chance of getting him to open up. The question is how do we get her next to him."

"Mildred Flowers." Albin said, settling the matter. "I'll call her."

One of the ultimate forms of magic is the ability to
have whatever you need before you realize you need
it."

—Donald M. Kraig, *Modern Magic*

Magic time

Three days later the uneasy alliance—Theo, Max, Effa,
and Albin—arrived at the grand old apartment building on lower Park Avenue where Mildred Flowers lived.
The doorman suddenly beamed: "Hello again, Mrs. Henneberg. Mrs. Flowers is expecting you and your guests."
Max shot Effa a puzzled look.

She simply smiled and thanked the man as he led them
through the lobby to a private elevator.

"I was here yesterday," she told the group as the elevator efficiently ground upward toward the penthouse floor.
"Nice man. Very protective."

In the living room, Shahid Patel, in a dark suit, a white
shirt, and modest striped tie, was planted on a huge sofa.
Mrs. Flowers sat in a claw-footed easy chair, the arms of
which ended with carved lion heads that almost smiled.
A small dark gold and very old Buddha in lotus position
took up most of a big mahogany sideboard. A soft herb-
al scent filled the room from a diminutive incense burner in front of the statue. The rest of the room was dim,
walls lined with bookshelves and paintings, small objects
on display tables, more seats. The two of them had been
drinking tea.

As a maid led them in, Shahid lept to his feet, his composure drained.

"What's this?" He wasn't sure who to ask.

"Don't worry my dear," Mrs. Flowers told him calmingly.

"You spoke to me about Moslem conceptions of matter and force," he replied accusingly. "Did you bring me here for this?" It was clear he realized too late, he'd accepted an invitation that had masked purposes.

"We knew you weren't a Buddhist," she returned with a bit of acid in her well modulated voice. "Do listen to us, please."

"You know me, Shahid," Effa began. "I'm Britz's mother. She called you when she was first disturbed about discrepancies in Miller's presentation. You know," she added seeing Patel's basically honest face twisting from the need to lie and lie again. "I didn't know until later that Dr. Miller had given Britz the same assignment he gave you and Karl."

"We're worried about Karl," Mrs. Flowers said. "Has he been heard from? It's been days and I believe the authorities are looking for him."

Patel sank back into the sofa and covered his face with his hands.

"It's probably just a matter of time," he mumbled into his hands. "State police, FBI." He looked up at the two women, his eyes full of pain. "I'm so shamed."

Max held Theo's arm and steered him away from the tea table to give space to the two women. Albin also removed himself by selecting a large brown velvet armchair across the room.

"I think you may have been one of the last people on earth to see my Britz alive." Effa's look was soft and insistent at the same time. She bent her head toward Patel. "The counterman at the luncheonette on Hudson Avenue saw you that Thursday night. You know he did."

"Yes," Mrs. Flowers added. "We know this too."

Effa opened her satchel to extract a bundle of pastel ribbons, rolled into a loose ball about the size of a softball. "The stones are over there," Mrs. Flowers told her. "River stones. "

Patel was clenching and unclenching his fists. He squeezed his eyes shut.

Effa moved to the left of Mildred Flowers' chair and the two women slowly linked their little fingers and curled the fingers on their opposite free hands.

"The truth will protect you. I'll see to it that it does." Mrs. Flowers had steely assurance in her voice. Her tone said she wasn't a person to be trifled with.

There was a long silence in which Mildred Flowers and Effa Henneberg hummed very softly, their odd tune together but in counterpoint. Max had to stop himself from rocking to the rhythm. He could feel Theo trembling through his shirt sleeve and a huge surge of affection for him filled Max like warm water.

"It was Karl. His terrible temper." Shahid spoke at last. "We were just supposed to get her papers and return them to the lab. He...he. She argued with him, Mrs. Flowers. I never thought he'd hurt her. When he did that, dear God..." Patel began chanting in Arabic, rocking back and forth as he did, while tears began rolling freely down his cheeks.

Mrs. Flowers kept steady. "Where was that?" she asked him.

"She was supposed to bring the papers with her, but she hadn't."

"Where was that?" Mrs. Flowers asked again.

"She said she'd meet me at this lunch place. But the counterman made us leave."

"On Hudson Avenue?" Mrs. Flowers asked, uncurling her right hand and placing it lightly on Patel's shoulder to slow his rocking.

"Yes, yes. So then we were out on the street. The guy inside was closing up. He didn't want us inside."

"Did you go somewhere else, Shahid?"

"We? No, Karl pushed her down an alley. He couldn't believe she didn't have the papers with her. He was yelling so loud. And then, and then, dear God, he picked her up and slammed her down onto the sidewalk."

"It was so fast. I didn't know what to do," Shahid sobbed. "I heard an awful snap. Broken neck I could tell. Her head was so bent. I just stood there. I was dead myself."

The silence in the room was almost as thick as swamp mud. Max clamped his teeth shut, hard. Albin stood ramrod stiff beside his seat. Only Theo seemed to be breathing; he emitted small noisy gasps. Effa and Mrs. Flowers now held each other around the waist swaying just a little.

Mrs. Flowers crooned almost inaudibly: "Poor man. How awful for you."

"How did her body get into the river?" Effa asked, just as softly.

"Karl picked her up. Put her over his shoulder. I

couldn't believe what had happened. I followed them. I threw her shoulder bag into the river. Karl tossed...just tossed. Her body went in. Like that. The water was going fast. Everything out to the harbor. Everything." He stopped. Effa stopped. Mrs. Flowers stopped and then handed Patel a large white napkin from the tea tray.

"My life is ended," he said into the napkin. "I've shamed everyone."

"Perhaps not," Mrs. Flowers counseled. "There are things to do. We need you to help the police. Did you two go back to see Dr. Miller?

"No, no, I couldn't. I just stayed in my room until I had to go to work on Monday. I haven't been faithful. I don't even have a mosque. Where could I go? I only knew I had to hide everything. Say nothing. Do nothing."

Shahid's tears of fright and repentance were being supplanted by tears of self-pity. Max watched the process taking hold, thinking an explosion would bring him relief. What it would be like to choke the life out of this whining coward? He could feel the muscles in his arms flexing and black bile rising in his throat. Mrs. Flowers caught his glare, shook her head, and he felt something go through his chest like a soft bolt of energy.

"You really are a witch, aren't you," he said to her after a moment. "Thank you."

§

It had been a very long afternoon. Conner had been summoned to Mrs. Flowers' house. So had Flemington Rivers, her attorney, and Dr. Miller. The tape recording

Effa had made was signed over to Conner. Rivers and Miller concluded deep arrangements, including how to brief the investors and the details needed to set up a renewed search for Karl. Miller would walk home, he said, shaking his head in mixture of relief and disbelief.

Then Conner, Rivers, and Patel headed together to the Manhattan House of Detention where Patel would be booked as a material witness.

"Not for long," Mrs. Flowers promised. "We'll post the bail if it is ordered. Flem here will be your advocate."

Mrs. Flowers' driver took the rest of them. Albin was let off on the Upper East Side. As neither Effa or Theo said anything to him as he left the car, Max followed suit. I wonder what that crafty bastard will be up to next, he was wondering. Were his thoughts loud enough for Effa to hear? She pulled away from him in the car and he knew he was being cut off. Theo was dropped on Avenue C. Then Max and Effa were carried over the Manhattan Bridge to Vinegar Hill in near total silence. When they reached Max's place Effa repaired to Max's bedroom.

About twenty-five minutes later she emerged. "I need a lift to the bus station," she announced, "or you could get me a car service." She was wearing her hat, mittens, poncho, boots and her packed backpack. Her satchel was on her arm. "I've spoken to the folks at New Harmony. They're fine about having me back."

"That's that?" Max spoke through a tight throat.

"I have to go now. I have to leave you. I have to go and work it through. I never, I never reconciled with..." She stopped, then pulled up to stand even taller than normal. "Aoife, Gondelieve, my dear lost daughter. I left so much

to others. I wanted to name her after me, but Albin object-
ed. I wanted her to be a new dawn, new light breaking.
Now I have so much work to do, for myself and for her.
But Max," she concluded, "thank you for being her soul
place. You gave her that and I'll always remember it."

She bent down to retrieve the backpack she'd set on
the floor.

"Well, if you're really leaving, call Theo will you?"
Max was slouched in the largest of his easy chairs. "I'm
punked to tell the truth."

Effa gave him a careful look: "You look peaked," she
agreed. "Are you hungry?"

"God no," he said. "I'm just done in."

If an injury has to be done to a man it should be so
severe that his vengeance need not be feared.
—Niccolo Machiavelli, *The Prince*

Pay back

It was morning two days later. The loft was empty. Even
the answering machine had quit blinking for the first
time in weeks. Had he been sleeping or not? His head
roared endlessly and every bone in his body ached as if he
hadn't slept for a week.

If this is depression, Max thought, no wonder it leads
to suicide.

I'll make myself eat something he decided even though
the thought of food made him feel queasy.

The street was as empty as usual but the day was shock-
ingly mild and the pungent smell of damp earth made Max
look up over the empty lots to the east. Sure enough he
could make out old man Balinski raking up winter debris
in a small empty lot near Water Street. Guess he thinks
it's really spring, Max thought. Come summer time most
of the space between the scattered still-standing buildings would be divvied up into uneven plots, designated
by impromptu fencing. They would host small crops of to-
matoes, dill, sweet peppers, and other vegetables favored
by the old time inhabitants and fiercely guarded by them.

Max pushed the door to the luncheonette open.

"You got a lotta nerve," Marty said, folding his arms
over his apron. "Whatja wanna see? How I did? Ja think
twenty-four hours in the slammer would turn *my* hair?"

Max's headache was worse than it had been out on the street.

"Marty?"

Christ, I should have thought it through before coming up here, a thought Max knew he was having much too late.

"Yeah. *'Marty.'*" His sarcasm pooled like syrup. "Suspicion they called it. You better believe Joe the Engineer's got your fuckin' name on a list. Get outta here. NOW!"

"Hey, hey," Max said. "What's going on?"

Tall Tiny was standing just behind Marty, looking just as hostile.

"A bust," Tiny said. "As if you don't know nothing."

"I know about the murder of my girlfriend. I know you guys have nothing to do with it." Max was holding onto the doorframe as the world slowly swung around and around him.

"Big Vinnie is on it now, you fuckin' Judas, so you better watch your little h'art studio. Somethin' tells me you could have a sudden accident in there. Something could start burnin'." Marty's Sicilian eyes were radiating black fury.

Max managed to walk away back down the street without doubling over. He had an intense pain in his middle. Gotta call Conner, he was telling himself, gotta call Conner. He threw up in the gutter just outside his gate. Burton and his buddy Eddy stopped on the steps to their door to watch the spectacle.

"Guess you heard about the raid on Big Vinnie," Burton snapped.

"No, nothing," Max answered, wiping his mouth on his sleeve. 'I'm fuckin sick, man."

"No surprise that," Eddy crowed. "Seems our local mobsters have some sort of card game scam and you've managed to totally fuck it up."

"Me?"

"That's what they told us. We enjoyed a personal visit from the big fat man's best buddies. Not our favorite thing." Burton had his hands on his hips broadcasting righteous indignation.

"Oh god," was all Max could muster.

"I don't know how you managed to upset them but we've always had the greatest respect for our locals. Don't like to think any one of us have caused them distress." Eddy's tone and posture was pure Burton.

"I think we made that clear," Burton concluded as Max unlocked his door and stumbled inside. Instead of Conner, he phoned Theo.

Run, run, as fast as you can
You can't catch me, I'm the Gingerbread man
I've run away from a little old woman
A little old man and
I can run away from you I can.
 —Traditional—with variations in Germany,
the British Isles, Eastern Europe, and the United States

RUN?

Theo arrived about an hour later, by which time Max had lapsed into a sick semi-sleep on one of the couches.

"Jeeze," Theo said slowly. Not only were all the living spaces disheveled but the studio was clearly deserted. No one had worked in there for days. A small pile of charcoal drawings had been left on the floor. A half sized canvas occupied the main painting wall. What was worse, all the art in the studio, even a mirror over the work sink, had been turned to the wall or covered over with drop cloths. It was bleak as Orthodox Jewish mourning.

"What's with you, man?" Theo peered into Max's face. "Jeeze," he repeated. "The whites of your eyes are as yellow as egg yolk. Are you poisoned?"

"I think I have hepatitis," Max mumbled.

"You been shooting? Max, no!"

"*Infectious* hep," Max replied. "Don't come too close to me and don't, don't." That was all he could say.

It didn't matter. Theo was already on the phone with Lois, asking her about doctors and hospitals in downtown Brooklyn.

At Downstate the first diagnosis was exactly the same as Theo's despite the lack of tracks on Max anywhere. Theo and Lois had to do monumental arguing, which finally required invoking the name of Max's gallery and the gallery's high-priced lawyer. In the end a staff gastroenterologist was called in and Max was given gamma globulin IV along with some badly needed saline for dehydration. Then, of course, the hospital wanted to admit him, "for observation." That entailed more argument which continued until the IV drip had restored some of Max's energy and he was able to check himself out "against medical advice."

"Lois, you're a life-saver," Theo told her as the two of them managed Max's semi-cooperative body out onto the street, where taxis waited. Her patient mastery of social work lingo had cut off several outbursts from Theo and some officious moralizing from a head nurse. Max had been given a vegan's nightmare list of diet requirements. In addition to the liver damage the virus had caused, Max had lost a great deal of weight as the infection took hold. Thus: calves liver every week, eggs and egg yolks, puddings all made with whole milk, no alcohol, no coffee. The litany extolled six small meals a day, cooked vegetables, cooked fruit.

"Theo, I have to leave," Max announced. "Not safe here," as his eyes closed.

"Not safe here," he repeated in the days following as friends filed in to see him. "They're not gonna let this stand," he tried to explain. His friends were relentlessly cheerful, some bringing forbidden beer, pies, chips, dips. Clipper showed up with a glistening mac 'n cheese casserole cooked by his new boyfriend. The Quorod Gallery sent a florist arrangement of candy and flowers in a large basket.

"They must think I sold something," Max said. "I have to leave," he said again.

Emily Transholm arrived at the end of the week bearing not food but two expensive art books on Charles Burchfield. Max perked up a bit wondering how she knew Burchfield's art or had guessed that the eccentric painter was a real favorite of his. He'd died only a few years before and now a museum for his once neglected works was opening in upstate New York.

She didn't say. Instead she had news about Karl. Karl was dead. Conner hadn't thought to call him about it, Max thought. I know I was sick but it's been weeks and I've heard nothing at all from Conner since he took off for the Tombs with Shahid, Mrs. Flowers, and her lawyer. I suppose for him the mystery part is solved and case settled if not closed. Getting Karl was never his business. Never his real care. Just another murder. Just another disconnected bureaucrat. Small wonder the poor schmo is so glum and downtrodden.

Emily shared the news: Karl had been cornered by the Border Patrol in a state park just outside Brownsville, Texas. His rental car had been identified on the way to the Matamoros Bridge but somehow the cops had bungled the stop. He'd been able to veer off the main road and had almost reached the Rio Grande through some wetlands, part of a large bird sanctuary adjacent to the state park.

"Karl had cash and contacts in Mexico," Emily told Max a bit breathlessly. "When his car got stuck in the swamp, he tried to run. The Border Patrol people said he was planning to swim for it. I don't doubt it for a minute. That man had a lot of faith in his physical prowess. The river isn't all that wide. A lot of drug traffickers try the same thing they told me."

"Shot dead?" Max asked. "They couldn't arrest him?"

"The whole thing hit us very hard," Emily said with a faint trace of bragging. "Dr. Miller's entire operation is being audited. He's left on a research exchange program in Munich. Six months. This will absolutely cool."

Well, she sure earned her paycheck, Max thought. But I'm out going to a trial and seeing that bastard sent to jail.

She went on: "No one is quite sure when Karl made his Mexican connections but apparently the plan was to bypass FDA approval, whether the drug received it or not. There would have been money to make selling a knock-off tPA to foreign markets."

"He was tossing his entire career for a quick buck?" There's more to this, Max was thinking but why should I care. "Was Patel in on it?" he asked suddenly feeling a return of the onset nausea of days before. She shook her head.

"He's in bad shape, poor man. Having some kind of breakdown. They've got him in Payne-Whitney for obser-vation."

All I need is him blabbing, Max was thinking, images of the encounter between Patel, Effa, and Emily Flowers spinning in his head.

"They tell me he'll be better in a week maybe two,"

Emily said, as Max slowly got up to see her out. "So will you. The worst is really over, Max."

At the door he noticed that a portion of the chain link fence separating his parking area from the street had been very neatly spliced. At least it looked that way.

§

"What's happening with your dad?" Max began when Theo dropped by to check on him that evening. Max wanted to talk about anything else before discussing the fence. It was clear to him he wasn't wrong. Big Vinnie and his people hadn't forgotten anything.

"I have no idea what that old bastard is up to." Theo started laughing. "He wanted to lay money on me. Get me involved in what he's calling the family enterprise! Last thing two things in the world he could tempt me with."

"What'd he say?"

"Oh he and his relatives have *huge* plans now. Entertainment. Some big deal about professional wrestling, about getting stadiums built, about paid TV for strip shows and God only knows. Seems everything's money for him now. His new religion? Anyway, he's gone. I think he went up to New England somewhere. That's where they all are."

"And what about Burton and Eddy. Anything more about that? About you and James Nexfield?"

"I owe James a lot," Theo said quietly. "I really used his love. There was love in his pages that'll always be in me. But Effa got it totally: it's my book and only mine. I haven't got anything to worry about."

"Okay. I do. They're just waiting to strike," Max said finally, sending Theo out to inspect the doctored fence.

"Neat job," Theo agreed when he returned. "Ya want me go out again and push all the garbage cans in front of that area? You'd hear it loud and clear if anyone tries to come through."

"Best not to let 'em know we even noticed," Max said resignedly.

They were sitting at the big kitchen table. Max closed his eyes. "Ya know, fuck it, make us a pot of coffee, Theo. The docs don't know everything."

"The lunch joint looks closed," Theo offered. "No lights, no cars in front. Nothing."

"So," said Max.

"Maybe they've closed shop, Max. I mean if the cops are watching, they'll have to find another place for their collections. They could've just left."

Max said nothing.

"Do you need a gun?" Theo asked.

Max shook his head. "Would you put something that cheesy in a story you'd write? Not to mention the little message they've left for me," he growled. "It says leave. They're gonna burn me out. Leave is their word. Leave is mine too. I'm not even giving you a key. Quorod'll look after the stuff here. If they want to."

"What are you saying? MAX!!"

"You're a bright guy."

"You gotta fight this. You can't let 'em drive you off!"

"It doesn't matter enough anyway. I'm empty. I can't work. I think I lost it a while back. It's all just empty shit. Not because Britz made me too fuckin' happy, Theo. It's just how it's been moving for me. I don't know any more."

"You *have* to work!"

"*You* have to work." Max raised his voice and clenched his fist. "I knew that way back about you. I'm not even leaving you a key," he repeated.

"I can't lose you, Max."

"Oh yes you can. I hear you're invited to give a reading at what, Salmagundi Club? I hear you're signing books up at Columbia. You've got a lotta work to watch your flank, work to figure out who to please, who you want to be with in the literary jungle. Most of all you've gotta work to *work*. God damnit. But me, I'm yellow now in more ways than one. I'm running out on all of it."

For a few years, MARTHA KING and her partner the painter/ poet Basil King owned half of an old house (and former bar) on Hudson Avenue in Vinegar Hill, Brooklyn. That was some ten years earlier than the 1980s in which this story is set. The first "Max" novel (*Max Sees Red*) was published by Spuyten Duyvil in 2019. She is currently working on a third (*Max Hates Blue*) and is grateful to Spuyten Duyvil who also published two collections of her short stories, *Little Tales of Family and War* and *North and South*.

For information about her other books and publications, please visit www.basilking-marthaking.com.